Ian Whybrow's
LITTLE WOLF'S BOOK OF BADNESS
ADAPTED BY ANTHONY CLARK

Sjerra

OBERON BOOKS
LONDON

This adaptation first published in 2007 by Oberon Books Ltd
521 Caledonian Road, London N7 9RH
Tel: 020 7607 3637 / Fax: 020 7607 3629
email: info@oberonbooks.com
www.oberonbooks.com

Little Wolf's Book of Badness © copyright Ian Whybrow 1995

Little Wolf's Book of Badness adaptation copyright © Anthony Clark 2007

A catalogue record for this book is available from the British Library.

Cover illustration by Tony Ross

ISBN: 978-1-84002-823-2

Printed in Great Britain by Antony Rowe Ltd, Chippenham.

This adaptation of Ian Whybrow's *Little Wolf's Book of Badness* by Anthony Clark, with original music by Conor Linehan, was first performed on 6 December 2007 at Hampstead Theatre with the following company:

GRIPPER / UNCLE BIGBAD, Grant Stimpson

GRIZZLE / LITTLE RED GOODIE-HOODIE, Ann Marcuson

LITTLE WOLF, Ilan Goodman

SMELLYBREFF / SCOUTMASTER, Christopher Staines

YELLER / MR TWISTER, Darell Brockis

SCOUTS, Sacha Buckley, Crispin Clark, Alex Cook, Chloe Evans, Julien Karim Jallane, Tilly O'Brien, Sara Tabar, Erica Seal, Kinnan Zaloom

Director, Anthony Clark

Musical Director, Duncan Wisbey

Choreographer, Matthew Bugg

Designer, Liz Cooke

Lighting Designer, Gregory Clarke

Company Manager, Kirsti Warwick

Deputy Stage Manager, Lucy Harkness

Assistant Stage Manager, Ali Hunter

Characters

LITTLE WOLF

SMELLYBREFF

YELLER

GRIPPER

GRIZZLE

UNCLE BIGBAD

MR TWISTER

SCOUTMASTER

SANJAY

DAVE

WOODCUTTER

LITTLE RED GOODIE-HOODIE

and

HUNTERS

BUS QUEUE

LITTLE MOUSE

STOAT

BUZZARDS

CUB SCOUTS

The play can be performed by an unlimited number of actors, but a minimum of five is required, with suggested doubling as follows:

ACTOR 1: Gripper / Uncle Bigbad / Buzzard 1 / Person In Queue / Echo / others

ACTOR 2: Grizzle / Woman / Echo / Little Red Goodie-Hoodie / Cub Scout / Little Mouse / Buzzard

ACTOR 3: Little Wolf

ACTOR 4: Smellybreff / Stoat / Field Creatures / Buzzard 2 / Scoutmaster / Person 2 / Echo

ACTOR 5: Yeller / Field Creatures / Person 1 / Mr Twister / Buzzard 3 / Woodcutter / Scout

Setting

Each scene should flow into the next with effortless fluidity. The actors should use props to create the various locations.

Costume

The style of the costume should reflect, where appropriate, Tony Ross's illustrations of Ian Whybrow's original book. Actors playing wolves should not have their faces covered.

Music

Where appropriate, the music should be performed live on stage by the actors. Dialogue in bold is sung.

Note

' / ' denotes overlapping dialogue – the point at which the next character starts speaking.

Part One

Music

The Lair. GRIPPER (Dad Wolf) writing a letter. GRIZZLE (Mum Wolf) preparing rabbit rolls and mice pies at a kitchen table.

GRIPPER: (*Writing.*) The Lair, Murkshire.

> *GRIPPER stops writing and stares at GRIZZLE. GRIZZLE stops what she is doing, looks up. Their eyes meet. She is about to say something when GRIPPER returns to his letter.*

Music continues – <u>Letter to Uncle Bigbad.</u>

GRIPPER: Dear brother Bigbad, are you well?
　　We haven't seen or heard from you for months.
　　We've written regularly but received no letters back.
　　We hope this doesn't mean you've got the sack?

　　We trust that you're still the Head of Cunning College?
　　Teaching wayward wolf cubs to be bad?
　　Is the old fox Mr Twister still running your affairs
　　Or have you both sold up for urban lairs?

　　Grizzle and I we're both being driven mad
　　Our eldest cub refuses to be bad,
　　He's growing up so clean and good, so very well-behaved
　　We're scared our reputation can't be saved.

　　He's far too nice to hang about this lair;
　　He always cleans his teeth and combs his hair;
　　He reads to his younger brother, sleeps all through the night;
　　His goody-good behaviour isn't right.

> *Enter SMELLYBREFF, coughing.*

GRIZZLE: You're up early, Smelly?

SMELLYBREFF: Little Wolf made me.

GRIPPER: Give us a growl!

SMELLYBREFF: And he made me brush my teeth, Mum!

GRIZZLE: Poor Smellybreff –

SMELLYBREFF: And I hate peppermint. Grrrr!

GRIPPER: Good growl.

GRIZZLE: (*Handing him a rabbit roll.*) Here, scoff this, get rid of the taste.

SMELLYBREFF: I wish he didn't have to live here.

GRIZZLE: You know you like your brother really. / Big burp, make it all better.

SMELLYBREFF: No I don't, he keeps trying to make me be good.

GRIZZLE: Scoff!

SMELLYBREFF eats.

GRIPPER: Don't you worry about Little. He's leaving home today.

GRIZZLE: Little Wolf is a bad cub at heart. / I know he is. It's just a phase, Gripper / – a phase he's going through.

**GRIPPER: Everything we've tried has come to nought
Our lair-life here is hideously fraught
Little needs an outside influence; he needs your wicked knowledge,
So please enrol our cub at Cunning College.**

**GRIZZLE: He's got the raw material like his dad,
To be very, very, very, very bad –**

**GRIPPER: But if his wolf potential isn't realised very soon,
He'll never hunt or howl at the waning moon.**

Enter YELLER with a kite.

YELLER: (*A good loud howl.*) Aarooo!

ALL: (*Howl back.*) AROOOO!

SMELLYBREFF: Hello Yeller.

YELLER: Hello Smellybreff. Where's Little?

SMELLYBREFF: Making his bed, and putting his clothes away.

YELLER: What's he doing that for? I've made us a kite.

SMELLYBREFF: Can I play?

GRIPPER: You can tell your cousin master Yeller, that there'll be no flying kites today.

YELLER: Why, Uncle Gripper?

GRIPPER: Fetch him here for me, Smelly.

SMELLYBREFF: He's got to go to College.

YELLER: College?

GRIZZLE: Shut up, Smelly.

GRIPPER: Yeller? / Go.

SMELLYBREFF: For being a goody-goody.

YELLER leaves. GRIPPER returns to his letter.

GRIPPER: **Remember brother our time at Brutal Hall,**
How we worked our sharp-claw paws off to be bad,
There were Nines Rules of Badness, that we practised day and night,
The badges to be won when we got them right!

GRIZZLE: **Our eldest Little's not a bit like you –**

GRIPPER: **Well, if he takes after you then you and me are through –**

GRIZZLE: **I know it seems unnatural, the way cubs behave today –**

GRIPPER: **Oh shut up we've agreed that the boy can't stay!**

SMELLYBREFF: Yeah!

GRIZZLE / GRIPPER: **Your nephew's a disgrace to the Bad Wolf pack,**
So, rough brute Brother Bigbad, don't hold back,
Show him how, make him aware, how wolves are born to scare,
Prepare him for life's trials beyond this lair.

GRIPPER: **If you are still Headmaster of Cunning College,**
Waive no fee – no favours – we will pay,
We want our Little Wolf back – a savage, fearsome beast
With mangy hair, sharp claws and yellow teeth.

GRIZZLE / GRIPPER: **Our Little needs to do some dirty deeds,**
To learn your bad habits and wicked ways,
We daren't forsake his future when we've tried so valiantly,
To bring him up as bad as a wolf should be.

ALL: **As bad, as bad, as bad, as bad**
We've tried so valiantly
As bad as bad as bad as bad
As bad as a wolf should be!
BRING HIM UP BAD!
BAD!

GRIPPER: (*Signing off the letter.*) Your anxious brother, Gripper.

GRIZZLE: He can't help himself being good.

GRIPPER: (*Helping himself to a pie.*) What do you mean he can't help himself; he's a wolf, isn't he? / These are yumshus.

GRIZZLE: He doesn't know who he is.

GRIPPER: He is furry of face and yellow of eye, sharp of teeth, and razor clawed, son of Grizzle the Headstrong and Gripper the Fierce. Feared throughout the County of Murkshire and beyond. Little sets a bad example / to his brother.

SMELLYBREFF: He does.

GRIZZLE: Smellybreff is more frightening than Little ever was at his age. Aren't you, Smelly? Where's that burp, then?

SMELLYBREFF: (*Burps.*)

GRIZZLE: That's better. And again.

SMELLYBREFF: (*Burps.*)

GRIZZLE: Get rid of all that nasty pepperminty toothpastey taste.

GRIPPER helps himself to a pie.

Paws off, or there'll be none left for greedy Uncle Bigbad.

GRIPPER: Yumshus.

GRIZZLE: I remember you saying it was your brother's unrivalled wolfy greediness that earned him the gold badge of badness… when you had to settle for silver.

GRIPPER: You fancied him didn't you?

GRIZZLE: He terrified me. What if he eats Little Wolf?

GRIPPER: He won't if Little is useful to him.

SMELLYBREFF: How can he be useful when he can't even hunt?

GRIZZLE: He hasn't had the practice.

GRIPPER: And whose fault is that?

GRIZZLE: Yours. You're the one that does all the hunting in this house.

GRIPPER: You're the one that feeds him.

Pause.

That's enough. We're sending him away to learn –

GRIZZLE: Yes, yes, I know…

GRIPPER: To hunt and be feared like his father, and his father's father, / father's father –

GRIZZLE: Yes, yes.

GRIPPER: Or he'll be trapped and skinned and turned into / slippers.

GRIZZLE: No, don't say that.

GRIPPER: Say what?

LITTLE WOLF and YELLER enter.

LITTLE WOLF: Good morning, Mum.

GRIPPER: No it's not.

GRIPPER is placing the letter in the envelope and licking it.

GRIZZLE: Give us a growl, there's a bad wolf.

LITTLE WOLF: Grrrr!

GRIPPER: Can't you do better than that, Little?!

GRIZZLE: (*Growls back.*) Grrr!

LITTLE WOLF: Grrr!

GRIPPER: Give your mother a growl to make her fur stand up!

LITTLE WOLF: Grrr!

GRIZZLE: / I'm frightened!

GRIPPER: / Pathetic.

GRIZZLE: Give us a howl, then.

YELLER: Arroo!

ALL EXCEPT YELLER: Blimey!

YELLER: My Mum says I'm loud for my age. I've always been loud and that's why I'm called Yeller.

SMELLYBREFF: And you've got yellow fur.

LITTLE WOLF: I don't see the point in howling and growling when there's no one to scare.

YELLER: You can scare Smelly.

LITTLE WOLF: But he's not annoying me.

SMELLYBREFF: I'll chew your toys.

LITTLE WOLF: Grrr!

GRIPPER: It's a cruel world out there, Little, full of human people who need scaring if you don't want them taking advantage. A wolf's growl is his first line of defence. Practise it!

LITTLE WOLF: Are we going on a picnic?

GRIZZLE: / Yes.

GRIPPER: / No.

LITTLE WOLF: Are we going to fly Yeller's kite?

GRIPPER: *We're* not going anywhere, Little.

LITTLE WOLF: Yeller made it from a packet of rat flakes. / Look, it's a wolf kite with yellow eyes.

SMELLYBREFF: Scary.

GRIZZLE: Little Wolf, your father and I have –

LITTLE WOLF: Please can I have a rabbit roll?

YELLER: / I hope it works.

GRIZZLE: / What did you say Little?

LITTLE WOLF: Please.

GRIZZLE: / No.

GRIPPER: (*Losing his temper and throwing a kitchen implement at him.*) What's with the pleases? Why can't you just snatch one like a normal cub?

LITTLE WOLF: Ow! Sorry.

GRIPPER: You will be if you keep apologising like a sissy. You'll snatch one, won't you Yeller?

YELLER snatches a pie or sandwich.

There, see, Yeller's wolf enough to snatch / a roll!

LITTLE WOLF: That's because you asked him to.

YELLER hands his pie to LITTLE WOLF.

(*To YELLER.*) Thank you.

GRIPPER and GRIZZLE growl in despair.

My Mum's rabbit rolls are the best.

GRIZZLE: (*To LITTLE WOLF.*) It's high time you learnt to kill your own rabbits, Little.

GRIPPER: (*Farts.*)

LITTLE WOLF: Excuse me!

GRIZZLE: (*Shocked.*) Little Wolf!

LITTLE WOLF: It wasn't me!

GRIPPER: What did you say?

LITTLE WOLF: Pardon me.

GRIPPER: What? / That was a stinky one.

LITTLE WOLF: I was only joking.

GRIPPER: How many times have I told you not to be so polite, Little?!

GRIZZLE: Get bad or your father'll mawl you!

LITTLE WOLF: No one shouts at Cousin Yeller when he's good.

GRIPPER: No one's going to be flying any kites today, Little, because today's the day you go to Cunning College to learn the Nine Rules of Badness.

LITTLE WOLF: Why?

GRIPPER: 'Proper bad' training is what you need.

GRIZZLE: Little, you must understand that before your Dad and I ever met, he had to train to be 'properly bad'... / That's how he got his silver Badge of Badness.

LITTLE WOLF: I can be bad when I want to be.

GRIPPER: Oh yes?

GRIZZLE: You'd like a Badness Badge though, wouldn't you?

LITTLE WOLF: Would I?

GRIZZLE: This will be an awfully big adventure for you, Little.

LITTLE WOLF: Who says?

GRIZZLE: And we're going to be so proud of you.

LITTLE WOLF: But what if I hate adventures?

GRIPPER: Cunning College for Brute Beasts is a good bad school. One of the best.

GRIZZLE: Do you remember your uncle?

LITTLE WOLF: No.

GRIPPER: Last time we saw Bigbad, Little was Smelly's age.

GRIZZLE: Your Uncle Bigbad is headmaster of Cunning College.

GRIPPER: Which is in the heart of Frettnin Forest, which is in the county of Beastshire, which is a long way away which means you're going to have to board.

LITTLE WOLF: Board?

GRIZZLE: You'll have to live there until you –

GRIPPER: A boarding school will be terrifying fun. It will help you concentrate on your studies.

GRIZZLE: See, Little, if you can't be better at being bad than your Dad. See if you can't win yourself a gold badge and make us all proud.

Silence.

(*Packing a rucksack.*) Oh don't be upset…we've talked about this…how the day would come…and now the day has come… It's high time you left this lair, you know it is…

LITTLE WOLF: Do I?

GRIPPER: You're a big wolf now.

SMELLYBREFF: I'm big too.

LITTLE WOLF: No I'm not.

GRIZZLE: Yes you are.

LITTLE WOLF: Then why do you call me Little?

GRIZZLE: Even when you're a big *bad* wolf you'll always be our Little.

LITTLE WOLF: But I can be bad at home –

GRIPPER: Here's a letter to Uncle Bigbad explaining everything, and a cheque to cover your fees, food and accommodation.

GRIZZLE: And make sure he feeds you half of everything you catch for him.

GRIPPER: You make sure you behave badly. My brother Bigbad will expect you to set a good bad example to the other brute beasts. Promise me you'll do that?

LITTLE WOLF: No.

GRIPPER: Promise me.

LITTLE WOLF: No, promises are good. / Got you!

GRIPPER: Grrr!

> *GRIPPER hands LITTLE WOLF his letter. LITTLE WOLF doesn't respond.*

LITTLE WOLF: How will I know what he looks like?

GRIPPER: (*Producing a WANTED poster.*) He's the cruellest, greediest, most fearsome wolf that ever prowled Beastshire. Here's an old WANTED poster he gave me. / He looks scary.

LITTLE WOLF: Wanted for what?

GRIZZLE: (*Fondly.*) The usual –

GRIPPER: Cruelty.

GRIZZLE: General wickedness.

GRIPPER: For being bad and proud of it.

LITTLE WOLF: But where is Cunning College?

GRIPPER: I said, it's right in the middle of Frettnin Forest.

LITTLE WOLF: Where's that? / And how am I going to get there?

GRIPPER: (*Producing a map.*) You can take my old map. Walk.

YELLER and LITTLE WOLF study the map.

LITTLE WOLF: Wow.

GRIZZLE: There's signs and symbols to represent the rivers and the roads –

LITTLE WOLF: (*Looking at the map.*) How long will it take?

GRIZZLE: There's a scale on it too, in the corner – six paws to the mile – down at the bottom, there…so, you can work out how far you've travelled each day.

GRIPPER: And how far you've got to go.

GRIZZLE: Do you see?

GRIPPER: Keep out of trouble and you should be there in a week.

GRIZZLE: Here's twenty-four rabbit rolls for the journey and a box of my finest mice pies to give to your greedy uncle. That's three rabbit rolls a day, and three spare just in case –

LITTLE WOLF: What if he's not there anymore?

GRIPPER: What if?

LITTLE WOLF: Uncle never answers your letters.

GRIZZLE: He probably never received them. It would take a brave postman to go anywhere near Cunning College.

LITTLE WOLF: And what if he attacks me?

GRIZZLE: Oh Little –

LITTLE WOLF: You don't care, do you?

GRIPPER: What if, what if, what if?

GRIZZLE: Of course we care.

GRIPPER: What if you go and find out how to be a real wolf cub before I lose my temper with you.

GRIZZLE: (*Handing LITTLE WOLF his rucksack.*) You know how we care Little…I've packed you two pairs of pyjamas, six pairs of pants, six pairs of socks…

LITTLE WOLF: I'm not ever going to change my clothes ever again…

GRIZZLE: …four shirts, two T-shirts, a change of trousers and a pair of tidy shoes…

LITTLE WOLF: Never ever again.

GRIZZLE: See, he knows how to be bad, Gripper…really he does.

LITTLE WOLF: I was only tricking being good.

SMELLYBREFF: Toothpaste was tricking.

LITTLE WOLF: You only care about Smellybreff. You don't care about me. He's your darling baby pet.

GRIZZLE: / We love you.

GRIPPER: That's enough!

GRIZZLE: (*Starts to cry.*) We're doing this for your own good.

LITTLE WOLF: No you're not.

GRIZZLE: Yes we are!

LITTLE WOLF: You're starting to drizzle, Mum.

GRIPPER: Put your pack on, Little Wolf?

Pause.

LITTLE WOLF: (*Pleading with GRIZZLE.*) I only cleaned my teeth for a joke, Mum. You ask Yeller, it was his idea.

YELLER: It wasn't.

LITTLE WOLF: Liar. One day you said let's pretend being good.

YELLER: I DIDN'T.

LITTLE WOLF: I remember you did.

YELLER: I didn't.

LITTLE WOLF: And then Mum you were supposed to say, 'Little Wolf you've gone barmy,' but you didn't and I was supposed to say, 'Arr harr, tricked you, I'm a bad boy really.' But now you're sending me away… I was only being good so you'd notice me.

Silence apart from the sound of GRIZZLE crying.

Music – <u>Goodbye Little Wolf</u>

ALL: **Goodbye Little Wolf, drizzle eye,**
Grizzle's cubs weren't born to cry,

Remember that we love you, remember that we care
Then 'wherever' won't seem far away,
From this dingy lair.

GRIZZLE, SMELLYBREFF and YELLER shift uneasily, all now about to cry, and giving LITTLE WOLF their various gifts.

GRIPPER: So long number one cub of mine,
Study hard and you'll soon find that you will know all nine,
Nine rules of Badness, and a gold badge you will win,
And then you'll be my pride and joy and real life can begin!

ALL: Goodbye Little Wolf, drizzle eye,
Grizzle's cubs weren't born to cry,
Remember that we love you, remember that we care
Then 'wherever' won't seem far away,
From this dingy lair.

Simultaneously spoken over the chorus:

GRIPPER: (*Handing him an exercise book.*) And here's one of my old exercise books for you to write the nine rules of badness / in.

GRIZZLE: So you don't forget them.

LITTLE WOLF: I'm not taking it.

GRIPPER: Take it.

GRIPPER hands his old exercise book to GRIZZLE to put in the rucksack.

SMELLYBREFF: Big bad Little Wolf, ta ta ra,
I'd like to come with you big bruv but Frettnin's far too far.
I'll stay behind and mess our den, and I'll try not to enjoy
Scribbling in your reading books and burying your toys.

ALL: Goodbye Little Wolf, drizzle eye,
Grizzle's cubs weren't born to cry,
Remember that we love you, remember that we care,
Then 'wherever' won't seem far away,
From this dingy lair.

Simultaneously spoken over the chorus:

SMELLYBREFF: I'm putting this torch in your rucksack.

LITTLE WOLF: Get off me.

GRIZZLE: You'll need it until your eyes get used to the dark.

LITTLE WOLF: I'll waste the batteries.

GRIZZLE: (*Bawls.*) Give him the torch, Smelly.

SMELLYBREFF: He doesn't want it.

GRIPPER: Give it to him.

SMELLYBREFF puts the torch in his rucksack.

YELLER: Farewell Little, Little farewell.
What the future holds for all us we can never foretell,
You may become a big bad wolf or fail at every turn
If badness's something Little Wolves just aren't supposed to
learn.

ALL: Goodbye Little Wolf, drizzle eye,
Grizzle's cubs weren't born to cry,
Remember that we love you, remember how we care
Then 'wherever' won't seem far away,
From this dingy lair.

Simultaneously spoken over the chorus:

YELLER: You can have my kite.

LITTLE WOLF: But it's yours. You made it.

YELLER: It will remind you of me because I'm your best friend. You
can make new best friends with it if you want. Everyone likes
flying kites.

LITTLE WOLF: What if they don't?

YELLER: You can use it to scare the buzzards on Parchin Plain.

LITTLE WOLF takes the kite.

GRIZZLE: It's all for the good, for the good of being bad,
We'll never forget you Little and fun times we've had,
This lair won't be the same dear cub especially at night,
So promise me my darling wolf you'll find the time to write!

ALL: Goodbye Little Wolf, drizzle eye,
Grizzle's cubs weren't born to cry,
Remember that we love you, remember how we care

Then 'wherever' won't seem far away,
From this dingy lair.

GRIZZLE: Here's some paper, and my favourite pen. You must write home everyday.

LITTLE WOLF: Just because writing is what I do best.

GRIPPER: Let us know how you're getting on with your badness. Try and make a few wicked friends, and remember: stay away from human people!

ALL: Goodbye Little Wolf, drizzle eye,
Grizzle's cubs weren't born to cry,
Remember that we love you, remember how we care
Then 'wherever' won't seem far away,
From this dingy lair
GOODBYE!

LITTLE WOLF takes a step. Stops. Silence.

Segue into <u>Travelling Music</u>

SCENE TWO

LITTLE WOLF takes two more steps, stops and opens the map.

SMELLY / YELLER: Walking is boring,
There's nothing to do

LITTLE WOLF: Except to keep walking,
Admiring the view.

GRIPPER / GRIZZLE: You've got to decide
What's the best route to take,

LITTLE WOLF: Should I follow the river,
Till I reach Lonesome Lake?

GRIPPER: (*Nods.*) You want to get beyond Lonesome Lake, through Spring Valley, and try and reach the town of Roaring River by the end of the day.

LITTLE WOLF: Do I?

SMELLYBREFF: That sounds a long, long way away.

GRIPPER: You can do it.

Travelling Music

LITTLE WOLF sets off.

LITTLE WOLF: **Stretching ahead**
And following me,
There's a dusty dirt track
Lined with tall chestnut trees.

Animals dart out of his way.

ALL: **The cats and field mice,**
The voles and the sheep,

LITTLE WOLF: **Dart out of my sight**

ALL: **At the sound of his feet.**

Consulting the map again.

LITTLE WOLF: **The further I walk**
Seems I'm further away

GRIPPER / GRIZZLE: **From the point you should reach**
At the end of the day.

LITTLE WOLF: **I'm fed up with walking**
My paws are all sore

ALL: **Here comes the night.**

LITTLE WOLF: **I can't walk any more.**
There isn't a town here,
It's still Lonesome Lake,
But I'm pitching my tent
'Cause I need a night's break.

He arrives at a signpost, with a life-ring attached, reading 'Lonesome Lake'. As the sun sets behind Lonesome Lake, LITTLE WOLF tries pitching his tent – unsuccessfully. Instrumental accompaniment.

This tent is stupid, it keeps falling down on purpose. I want to go home!

I'm feeling so lairsick,
What would make me feel better
Would be to eat my three rolls, Mum,
And I write you a letter.

LITTLE WOLF sits on his map and writes his first letter.

'Dear Mum and Dad, Please please / PLEEZE let me come home!'

SCENE THREE

The Lair. GRIPPER and GRIZZLE reading from a pile of letters. SMELLYBREFF scribbling in LITTLE WOLF's books.

GRIZZLE: (*Reading; overlapping with LITTLE WOLF.*) 'Please please PLEEZE' – spelt P, L, double E, Z, E. Let me come home. Pleeze let me come back and be bad at home.'

SMELLYBREFF: No please.

LITTLE WOLF: (*Writing.*) 'The sun is falling in the water. The moon is coming up. I can just see my pen and paper but I wish it was brighter. Camping is the worst thing.' (*Looking at the map.*) And this stupid map says I am sixty paws away from you and there's another seven hundred more paws to go, maybe more… I am frozz, I am hopeless.

GRIZZLE: (*Reading.*) 'Yours tired-outly, Little –'

LITTLE WOLF: '– Wolf.'

SMELLYBREFF yawns.

GRIZZLE: Grrr, that was only Day One.

Travelling Music

Bright sunlight. LITTLE WOLF packed and up on his feet.

LITTLE WOLF: **Walking is boring**
When I can still see
More Lake on this side,
On this side more trees.

If I reach Hilly End
By the end of the day,
I'll have walked the same distance,
I walked yesterday.

You've got it all wrong, Dad,
It'll take more than a week

To reach Cunning School
With raw paw sore feet.

If I run out of food,
What am I going to do?
You can't expect me to hunt
When I haven't a clue?

I know you don't care
But I didn't want to come
For this walk in the first place
And told you so, Mum?

Here comes a new night,
And my whole body kills,
I'm going to stop here,
Now I've reached the Nine Hills.

LITTLE WOLF sits down to write another letter.

GRIPPER: (*Referring to the second letter.*) 'Up the Hilly End of Lonesome Lake. Day Two.' What's he been doing?

GRIZZLE: He's not used to roaming so far, Gripper. Just because you walked the nine counties at his age, doesn't mean... / Poor Little. More Ratflakes Smelly? Goosabix? Voletarts?

SMELLYBREFF with his face in a bowl.

GRIPPER: He shouldn't have taken the long way around the lake. Listen to this. I think he's walking slowly on purpose. (*Reading.*) 'You won't make Smellybreff –'

LITTLE WOLF: (*Writing.*) '– leave home when he is my age.'

SMELLYBREFF: I want to watch the telly.

LITTLE WOLF / GRIPPER: 'You will just say –'

GRIZZLE: Oh yes, / darling pet.

LITTLE WOLF: 'Oh yes darling baby pet. You may stay here safe with us and watch telly all you want.' And what about Yeller?

GRIPPER: We don't spoil Smellybreff.

GRIZZLE: We don't.

LITTLE WOLF: (*Writing.*) 'Yeller says pardon when he burps.'

GRIPPER: (*Reading.*) 'And his parents –'

LITTLE WOLF: (*Writing.*) '– don't send him to school in a faraway forest.'

GRIZZLE: He's right.

GRIPPER: Yeller's parents don't mind him being a softy…'Yours fed-uply –'

LITTLE WOLF: / 'Little –'

GRIPPER: 'Little Wolf.'

Bright sunlight. LITTLE WOLF packed and up on his feet.

Travelling Music

LITTLE WOLF: (***Walking.***) **Walking is boring,**
There's nothing to do
Except to keep walking,
Admiring the view.

GRIZZLE: (*Reading.*) 'Spring Valley. Day Three.'

GRIPPER: He still hasn't crossed the river then?

GRIZZLE: Don't worry, he'll soon be in Beastshire.

Travelling Music

LITTLE WOLF: **I imagine ten wolf packs**
All laughing at me,
As the leaves in tall trees
Gently sway in the breeze.

LITTLE WOLF avoids two hunters.

And me in my turn I
Must hide when I see
Hunters with guns
Who are looking for me.

LITTLE WOLF hiding, writing a letter.

GRIZZLE: (*Reading.*) 'Dear Mum and Dad –'

LITTLE WOLF: '– Aaah, the hunters got me in Lonesome Woods, urg.'

GRIZZLE: (*Dropping the letter.*) Oh dear!

GRIPPER: (*Snatching up the letter and reading.*) 'Only kidding, I am all right really. Had you worried. Sad to say, but I have eaten most of Mum's rabbit rolls already. Boo, shame. Will get to a town called Roaring River tomorrow. Yours tired-outly, Little Wolf.'

GRIZZLE: He's sounding more like himself, then?

GRIPPER: He is. Where's Smelly got to?

Back in the open. LITTLE WOLF walking.

Travelling Music

LITTLE WOLF: (*Consulting the map.*) I'm trudging Spring Valley
To bridge number five,
Which I'll cross to the town
Where I hope I'll survive.

When I was a baby,
All podgy and sweet,
Mum said stay clear of people
You meet in the street.

The sounds and movement of a busy town.

This town's full of dangers
You said I would meet,
So I'll skirt through the outskirts,
Catch a bus to Crow's Feet.

LITTLE WOLF writing a letter in a bus shelter.

GRIPPER: (*Reading.*) 'Day Four. Roaring River. Dear Mum and Dad, there are so many people here you would not believe. I like buses, they are smelly and good growlers. People line up and get inside them. It's funny, just like Dad eating sausages. This morning I wanted to be a sausage.'

Travelling Music

PERSON 2 joins LITTLE WOLF in the shelter.

LITTLE WOLF: Can I catch a bus
To Crow's Feet from here?

PERSON 2: If you want the number thirteen,
Better queue with us here.

LITTLE WOLF joins a queue but doesn't know the form.

PERSON 1: **Young man, you must get**
   To the back of the queue,
   There's people stood there
   Who were here before you.

LITTLE WOLF joins the end of the queue.

LITTLE WOLF: **When is it coming?**

WOMAN: **I say, is that a fur?**
   If it is take it off
   Or my wrath you'll incur.

LITTLE WOLF: I can't.

WOMAN: (*Hits him with her basket.*) Take that for animal rights!

   All creatures on earth
   Have their own right to live,
   We have no right kill them
   It's insensitive.

LITTLE WOLF: Stop! Stop hitting me!

WOMAN: **Take off that coat**
   You excuse for a man,
   How dare you upset
   Our Creator's great plan...

WOMAN hitting him more violently.

LITTLE WOLF: But I am an animal.

WOMAN: What sort of an animal?

LITTLE WOLF: A wolf.

WOMAN: (*Screams.*) A wolf? Wolf, everybody!! Wolf! Wolf!

WOMAN runs off followed by the others. LITTLE WOLF eats the contents of her shopping basket.

GRIPPER: (*Reading.*) 'So there you are, everybody else thinks I'm bad, even if you think I'm Goodie Four-Paws. Remember when Mum was asleep that time and I nipped off her whiskers with the claw clippers?'

GRIZZLE: I remember all right. I had to wear fake whiskers for weeks.

GRIPPER: (*Reading.*) 'And what about the time I glued Smellybreff's tail to his chair?'

SMELLYBREFF: Ow!

LITTLE WOLF opening a box of soap powder.

GRIPPER: Listen to this, he's found himself some food without having to hunt for it!

GRIZZLE: Clever Little!

GRIPPER: Not so clever. Listen. (*Reading.*) 'Her shopping was quite tasty except for some white powdery stuff in a box. It made my tongue go bubbly… Yours spittingly, Little Wolf.'

The sound of a distant train or two. LITTLE WOLF emerging from a cloud of bubbles reading the map.

Travelling Music

LITTLE WOLF: I must now take the steep path
From Crow's Feet Crossroads,
To climb Murky Mountain
All covered in snow.

LITTLE WOLF starts to climb the mountain

From up here the houses
Look like small sparrow's nests,
The roads look like veins,
And the cars hum like pests.

The sound of another distant train.

This path leads me round
As I climb higher and higher,
And there's a howl in the valley
That reminds me of Yeller.

Yeller! Is that you Yeller? Come to fetch me home?

It's only a train,
And I'm calling in vain,
It would be very nice, friend,
To see you again.

The path's getting steeper,
There's a fog in the air,
It's cold, getting colder.
I'm feeling quite scared.

GRIPPER: (*Reading.*) 'Somewhere Rocky. Day Six. You have to climb up and up so high where nothing grows, not even trees. Murky Mountains are very dangerous.'

<u>Travelling Music</u>

LITTLE WOLF: **Best paw put forward,**
Paw left right, right left,
The path's getting slippery,
I'm losing my breath.

GRIPPER: (*Reading.*) 'Two times I nearly skidded over the edge of the path.'

LITTLE WOLF: **Walking is hard now**
There's ice on the ground,
This path's leading nowhere
I'm going round and round.

LITTLE WOLF writes on the mountain wall 'Trick Path'.

GRIPPER: (*Reading.*) 'I got lost.'

GRIZZLE: No.

GRIPPER: (*Reading.*) 'My breath was white clouds. Then I saw a deep dark tunnel going into the mountain. My fur started jumping up all along my back, and a sign above the entrance read –'

LITTLE WOLF: (*Reading.*) 'Borderlands Tunnel to Borderlands Market – No U-turns – No Stopping – No Way Back – FRETTNIN FOREST 58 miles.' The scares start here.

GRIPPER: 'But I didn't want to stay in the open and freeze.'

LITTLE WOLF: Can't scare me.

LITTLE WOLF dives into the tunnel.

Blackout.

Music – <u>Running in the Tunnel</u>

Yellow eyes are friends with the dark!

ECHO: Yellow eyes are friends with the dark-ark-ark-ark…

Music describes LITTLE WOLF's journey in the tunnel.

GRIZZLE: Turn your torch on, Little, turn your torch on!

GRIPPER: You're not scared are you, Little, it's only a tunnel!

LITTLE WOLF: I'm holding my breath!

GRIZZLE: Little!

GRIPPER: Little!

LITTLE WOLF switches his torch on.

GRIZZLE: Little!

Segue into <u>Borderlands Market Rag</u>

Lights up.

LITTLE WOLF has emerged from the tunnel in Borderlands Market. The moon shines down.

LITTLE WOLF: Phew! Moonshine at last! Not far to go now!

LITTLE WOLF settles down and eats his rolls and writes.

GRIPPER: (*Reading.*) 'It was the best feeling ever to be in the open, looking at the moon shining down. It was shining on Borderlands Market.'

LITTLE WOLF: Can't keep awake.

GRIZZLE: Brave Little.

GRIPPER: (*Reading.*) 'More tomorrow.'

GRIZZLE: How many rolls has he got left?

GRIZZLE: Gripper?

GRIPPER: Six.

GRIZZLE: How many days before he gets there?

GRIPPER: At his rate…at least four.

GRIZZLE: What are we going to do, he'll starve!

Music – <u>Travelling Music</u>

LITTLE WOLF: Walking is tiring,
I've still got sore paw,

**I'm falling asleep now
I can't walk anymore…**

LITTLE WOLF: (*Signing off.*) 'L.'

GRIPPER: 'L.'

GRIZZLE: Just L? No love?

GRIPPER: No love. Just L.

He settles down under a market stall. Lights fade. Beat.

SCENE FOUR

Travelling Music

Lights up. Morning. A busy market. MR TWISTER discovers LITTLE WOLF.

MR TWISTER: (*In LITTLE WOLF's ear.*) My boy!

LITTLE WOLF: Ooo-er, a fox!

MR TWISTER: Mister Twister is my name, and you are camping under my stall.

LITTLE WOLF: I didn't know it was yours. / I –

MR TWISTER: Do not worry yourself, my boy. There will be no charge. Something tells me you are a keen young chappie who is eager to assist me with my work today. You can help me sell these dressing up clothes.

Opening up his costume / fancy dress hire stall. Clothes, fake noses, false hair, wigs, coconut shells, wings etc.

Music – Twister Disguises

**Try Twister Enterprises,
For this country's best disguises,
If you're looking for that new someone to be!
You know we cater for all sizes
Here at Twister's bold Disguises,
We'll help you find
A new identity!**

**When you're going to a party
And they say it's fancy dress
And you need that special costume to impress,**

No one believes their eye-zes
No, they'll never realise,
You're bound to win
First prize in this disguise.

When you see our wide collection
Of false beards and permed moustaches,
And you're trying on our wigs and glasses range,
You take Twister's sound advice,
Choose to wear his merchandise,
And he'll guarantee it all
At bargain prices.

Enter LITTLE MOUSE.

LITTLE MOUSE: Sir, I'm feeling so, so lonely,
    Could you help to recommend me
    Something nice that I might wear to make best friends?

LITTLE WOLF: If you stand upon your head, sweet mouse,
    And try these plastic wings,
    You could be a blind fruitbat,
    Do you fancy that?

LITTLE MOUSE: Sir, if loads of bats play games with me
    And I can join a colony
    I'll squeak and flap
    Like any type of bat.

LIITLE WOLF: Then close your beady eyes, sweet mouse,
    And practise batty cries,
    I will ties these wings on tight
    And give you the gift of flight.

LITTLE MOUSE: Make sure you tie them good and tight,
    I've never flown before,
    And I'm nervous I'll take off
    And hit the floor...

LITTLE WOLF: Do not worry but don't forget
    To flap your mousey paws,
    You'll make a class fruitbat
    If you remember that.

LITTLE MOUSE: **Can I swap them for some fishy fins**
   If these wings don't feel right?
   I may be better at swimming than I am at...

Instrumental section, as LITTLE MOUSE is launched into the air.

LITTLE WOLF: You look superb!

LITTLE MOUSE lands flat on his face.

MR TWISTER: You'll soon master it. Practise, that's all.

LITTLE MOUSE: I'd like two pairs please!

LITTLE MOUSE pays up.

Enter a STOAT.

STOAT: **I'm going to a party,**
   And they say it's fancy dress,
   So I'm seeking something weird
   That I can wear?
   I don't like competition,
   But beside the party guests
   I want to cut a dash
   Above the rest.

LITTLE WOLF: **You do present a problem,**
   You're all back and tiny bum,
   But I've a great idea what you could be.
   If you shaved off all your fur, dear stoat,
   And wore this nutty shell,
   You'd be a garden tortoise
   And do well.

STOAT: Good idea! How much do you want?

MR TWISTER: (*Whispering to LITTLE WOLF.*) Double it.

LITTLE WOLF: Double what you're offering.

STOAT: Half again, how's that?

MR TWISTER: All right.

LIITLE WOLF: Three quarters.

STOAT: Done. Tie it up!

LITTLE WOLF ties the shell on the STOAT, who can't keep still.

LITTLE WOLF: Stay still!

STOAT: How do I look? Show me.

LITTLE WOLF shows STOAT himself in the mirror.

Like a tortoise.

LITTLE WOLF: You've got to slow down, or no one will believe you.

STOAT wobbles his head and pads about like a tortoise.

MR TWISTER / LITTLE WOLF: **When you look into your mirror**
And you feel the need to be
Something other than the person that you see,
Try Twister's bold Disguises
For that new identity,
We will help you change
Your personality.

When you're going to a party
And they say it's fancy dress
And you need that special costume to impress,
Try Twister Enterprises
For our range of styles and sizes,
If you want to win first prize
For best disguise.

Try Twister Enterprises,
For this country's best disguises,
If you're looking for a new someone to be!
Try Twister's bold Disguises,
For our range of costume sizes,
We will help you choose
A new identity!

We will help you choose
A NEW IDENTITY!

MR TWISTER: You're a good little worker. I might like you to stay and be my full-time dresser-upper, and one day you never know, you might have a stall of your own.

LITTLE WOLF: Thank you, Mister Twister, but I'm on my way to Cunning College.

MR TWISTER: Cunning College, Frettnin Forest?

LITTLE WOLF: Yes, do you know it? Mum and Dad want me to get my Bad Badge.

MR TWISTER: My boy, I was a teacher there many a full moon ago.

LITTLE WOLF: My Uncle Bigbad is Headmaster.

MR TWISTER: What? You? The nephew of that horrid crook Bigbad?

LITTLE WOLF: (*Proudly.*) Yes.

MR TWISTER: I first met your uncle at Broken Tooth Caves. We were both holed up there, running from the police. Then he had the bright idea we could hide in Frettnin Forest and start up a school for brute beasts. It was my idea to call it Cunning College. And he promised me that if I was prepared to invest my loot, and work hard helping him teach the naughty pupils to be even naughtier, I would soon be very, very rich...

LITTLE WOLF: What is Cunning College like?

MR TWISTER: My boy it was dreadful. The pupils never gave me a moment's peace! They were most awfully sly and squirmy, all those little skunks and stoats, rattlesnakes and cubs! How they got on my nerves, those spoilt little brutes. And what a fuss their horrid parents made, always asking when their ghastly offspring would be getting their Bad Badges! They quite wore me out. Are your parents like that? And when I asked your uncle for some money – my money, mind, hard-earned – just enough to allow me to take a short holiday, he threatened to eat me!

LITTLE WOLF: What did he say?

MR TWISTER: He never paid me. He told me to get out and said that if I ever put a paw in his school again, he would boil my bones and serve me up as soup. You see, your uncle's a thief and a miser. He is Mister Mean. He has bags of money hidden away but he will not part with a penny. And he's dangerous, because he has a terrible temper. My strong advice to you, my boy, is STAY AWAY from Cunning College!

LITTLE WOLF: Oo-er!

MR TWISTER: Believe me you will never be his special pupil, you'll be a sausage in a sandwich. Stay here with me.

LITTLE WOLF: But how am I going to get my Bad Badge and keep up the good name of wolf, if my uncle is going to eat me?

MR TWISTER: Your uncle owes me half his fortune. And it's in that college somewhere, I know it is. One day I'm going to reclaim it.

LITTLE WOLF: Maybe he has changed since you left, and what if I asked him kindly for the money he owes you and brought it back to you on my way home?

MR TWISTER: It wouldn't work. Look into my eyes! You could make your fortuney...tune here. Stay here with Mister Twister...

LITTLE WOLF: (*Dreamily.*) Will you pay me?

MR TWISTER: Young chappie, you owe me for taking shelter under my stall, and for saving you from a terrible fate. Now get to work. Tidy up those bonnets, while I go and have my breakfast. We'll be busy today I know we will.

Music – <u>Twister Disguises</u>

MR TWISTER leaves. LITTLE WOLF hangs up the bonnets and tidies the stall.

SCENE FIVE

Back in the Lair, Murkshire.

GRIZZLE: 'Dear Mum and Dad, I am a bit bothered. I have met Mister Twister, Uncle Bigbad's not-any-more business partner. He works in Borderlands Market selling dressing-up clothes and he says terrible things about Uncle, and says I should stay with him and work and be his dresser-upper forever. One minute I think I will and become very, very rich, and then the next I remember you and about how I need to be learning the Nine Rules of Badness.'

GRIPPER: What's he doing? He's not going to give up when he's so close?

GRIZZLE: It says here, 'I want you to be proud of me. I have a small wolfy plan –'

In Borderlands Market. LITTLE WOLF puts on an old woman's bonnet and cloak. MR TWISTER reappears.

MR TWISTER: Good morning, Madam, can I help?

LITTLE WOLF: (*As an old woman.*) Yes.

MR TWISTER: I'm sorry have you been waiting long? My assistant – Where's he got to – ?

LITTLE WOLF: (*As an old woman.*) Don't worry, he sold me this magnificent bonnet.

MR TWISTER: It makes you look very old, Madam.

LITTLE WOLF: (*As an old woman.*) If I look older than I am that's good because nobody takes me seriously. I asked your assistant whether he knew the way to Parchin Plain because I've got a friend I'm supposed to be meeting there – and he said you would know, Mister Twister, if your name is Mister Twister, and he went off looking for you…

MR TWISTER: Of course, of course… Straight ahead, left at the crossroads and… You keep that bonnet on, or the sun will fry you alive. It's baking out there. Hope you meet your friend.

LITTLE WOLF walks off.

(*Calling for his assistant.*) Little Wolf! Little Wolf! Where are you? Come here! How much did you charge the old lady for the bonnet?

MR TWISTER leaves.

SCENE SIX

Travelling Music

LITTLE WOLF walks away, the market disappears, and he finds himself walking across The Parching Plain. He stops to write a letter.

LITTLE WOLF: 'Dear Mum and Dad, I slipped away from Borderlands Market…'

In the same playing space, to one side, above or below, GRIPPER and GRIZZLE are reading a letter.

GRIPPER: 'The Parching Plain. Day Nine.'

GRIZZLE: Day Nine?!

GRIPPER: (*Reading.*) 'Disgizzed, discussed –'

GRIZZLE: I think he means '*disguised* as an old lady, I'm going on for your sake.'

GRIPPER: And for your own sake, Little.

GRIZZLE: I'm so proud of you.

GRIPPER: Dreadful writing.

GRIZZLE: Just like yours.

LITTLE WOLF: 'The / land is flat…'

GRIPPER: 'Land is flat with no shade for miles and miles…'

LITTLE WOLF takes off his bonnet, mops his brow.

(*Reading.*) 'Some birds as big as planes are gliding round and round way up high above me.'

Music – <u>The Song of Four Buzzards</u>

BUZZARDS appear. As they sing they swoop on LITTLE WOLF.

BUZZARDS: **Come, let's soar up high**
In an azure blue sky,
Let's spread out our wings
And forget we can fly.

Let's glide round in circles
Above Parchin Plain
And keep our eyes scanned
On the desert terrain.

We're the buzzards of Beastshire
We're all beak and claw,
We're the cruellest of all your
Big bird predators.

BUZZARD 1: **Do you see what I see?**

BUZZARD 2: **I can see it okay.**

BUZZARD 1: **A Little Bad Wolf**

BUZZARD 2: **That has wandered astray.**

BUZZARDS: The path of his footprints
　　Is crooked and deep
　　And he's starting to stagger
　　As he falls asleep.

　　We're the buzzards of Beastshire
　　We glide round and round,
　　Then we'll swoop on our prey
　　As it falls to the ground.

LITTLE WOLF staggers and falls in the sand.

BUZZARD 1: Come buzzard, come buzzard!
　　And feel the rush and the thrill,
　　As our poor prey lies stranded,
　　Let's dive in for the kill.

The BUZZARDS swoop down and peck at LITTLE WOLF as he stumbles.

LITTLE WOLF: Go away! Leave me alone.

Instrumental section as the BUZZARDS peck at LITTLE WOLF. He bats them out of the way, shouting at them. Then he gets the idea to use YELLER's kite to scatter them. LITTLE WOLF unpacks, unfurls and flies the kite. The music soars.

BUZZARD 1: Did you see?

BUZZARD 2: What I saw?

BUZZARD 1: Come to ruin our feast!
　　A bright yellow-eyed thing

BUZZARD 1 / 2: A flat, flying beast!

LITTLE WOLF: Kite fly, fly up high,
　　Scare those buzzards away,
　　I'm not going to give up
　　To be their next prey.

　　I'm a wolf!

BUZZARD 2: I'm a bird!

LITTLE WOLF: I'm not scared of you!

BUZZARD 2: We could peck you alive.

LITTLE WOLF: **I could gnash you up too.**

The BUZZARDS and the kite fight. Much swooping and dancing. The BUZZARDS retreat every time they see the wolf eyes on the kite.

BUZZARD 1: **Buzzards of Beastshire,**
Let's sound the retreat!
In the face of those eyes,
We acknowledge defeat!

The BUZZARDS sound a retreat, and retreat.

LITTLE WOLF: **Thanks, cousin Yeller,**
For saving my life,
Your kite gave the Buzzards
One hell of a fright!

Thanks, cousin Yeller,
Thank you!

LITTLE WOLF glides across the plain, holding tight to the string of his kite, eventually coming to edge of Frettnin Forest, where he lets it go.

GRIZZLE: 'I am posting this on the edge of Frettnin Forest. It looks darker in there than the Borderlands Tunnel. Spooky. I have eaten all my rabbit rolls. This could be my last letter. Ever.'

Music – A soundscape of mysterious Frettnin Forest noises

GRIZZLE bursts into tears.

LITTLE WOLF: (*Whistles.*)

SCENE SEVEN

Through the undergrowth the schoolhouse door appears. In the beam of LITTLE WOLF's torch, a sign reads:

CUNNING COLLEGE. BADGES AWARDED FOR WICKED WAYS, DIRTY DEEDS & BAD HABITS.

A bell rope to one side. LITTLE WOLF pulls the rope. The bell rings.

Music – <u>Bigbad Theme</u>

After a time the sound of footsteps walking a long corridor. The door opens, it creaks on its hinges.

UNCLE BIGBAD stands in the doorway. Very, very tall – on stilts. He wears his gold Badness Badge.

LITTLE WOLF: H-h-h-hello Uncle Badbiggy, I am your n-nephew L-Little Wolf. M-Mum and Dad sent me so you can t-teach me the Nine Rules of B-Badness.

UNCLE BIGBAD: Grrrrrr! BE GONE VILE BALL OF FLUFF! Fly and flee or I'll fetch a vacuum cleaner and hoover you up.

LITTLE WOLF: B-b-but I am your nephew. (*Handing him a letter.*) Here is a letter from your brother Gripper, my Dad.

UNCLE BIGBAD: How nice, a letter! Just because I ate the postman no one delivers me post anymore. Stand still while I pepper and salt you!

He puts his hands in his pockets and pulls out a large pepper and salt.

LITTLE WOLF: Mum said you'd be hungry, which is why she's made you some nice mice pies. They may be stale but they'll still taste nicer than me.

LITTLE WOLF pulls a couple of pies out of his bag.

UNCLE BIGBAD: Sniff snuff sny! I smell pie! Give them to me swiftly, swiftly!

LITTLE WOLF: You can have them, if you promise to teach me –

UNCLE BIGBAD: Give them to me!

Grabbing the two pies and slamming the door shut.

LITTLE WOLF: Wait a minute! Uncle, that's not fair. Mum and Dad – Open the door!

I've got more pies if you want.

(*Shouting through the letter box.*) If you want more, just open the door!

The door opens.

UNCLE BIGBAD: Sniff snuff sny! I smell more pie!? Did you say you had some more? Give them to me before I eat you –

LITTLE WOLF sneaks between UNCLE BIGBAD's legs and disappears into the college.

Give them to me, you rascal!

LITTLE WOLF: Only if you promise to teach me the Nine Rules of Badness.

UNCLE BIGBAD: Yes, yes, yes! Now GIVE ME YOUR PIES! YOUR PIES OR YOUR LIFE YOU LITTLE DIMP!

GRRRRRR!

The music rises. Blackout.

Part Two

Music – <u>Bigbad Theme</u>

Inside Cunning College. Dust and cobwebs. UNCLE BIGBAD sitting on a desk. LITTLE WOLF standing on a chair holding out a mice pie for him. UNCLE BIGBAD makes a swipe at it but LITTLE WOLF pulls it away just in time.

UNCLE BIGBAD: Listen, you vile ball of fluff, you can clean the blackboard, flit the flies, polish the desks, shoo the spiders, and lick the lavs –

LITTLE WOLF: I thought we were supposed to be doing badness!

UNCLE BIGBAD: Small wolves clean up, big wolves sit down, eat and watch the telly.

LITTLE WOLF: Why are you so huffy and puffy? I thought you were supposed to be a great teacher. Don't you want to teach me?

Music – <u>Sniff Snuff Sny</u>

UNCLE BIGBAD: Sniff snuff sny
    I smell mouse pie,
    Don't play silly games with me
    When food's in short supply.
    There'll be no badge, you won't succeed,
    Unless you start to feed my greed,
    You'd better give me all you've got
    Before I poach you in my pot,
    You're the only one that's left here now
    To keep me satisfied.

LITTLE WOLF: Where have they all gone?

UNCLE BIGBAD: Where do you think?

    Sniff snuff sny
    I want your mice pie!
    Hand me what you've got right now
    Or else I'll make you cry.
    I'm head of school my young nephew,

> You'll do the things I want you to,
> It's cruel to wave those lovely pies
> In front of my sad hungry eyes,
> No rules for you until I'm fed
> Or else straight up to bed.

Swiftly, swiftly! Paw it over!

LITTLE WOLF: No! (*Holding a pie out to him.*) Not until you teach me the Nine Rules of Badness

UNCLE BIGBAD: **Sniff snuff sny**
> **I see good mice pie,**
> **Don't you dare deny me them**
> **Or be prepared to die.**
> **Mice pie, feed me, swiftly feed me**
> **Bargaining won't do,**
> **I don't care who you say you are**
> **I'm fond of nephew stew.**

LITTLE WOLF: If you kill me, my Dad will kill you.

UNCLE BIGBAD: Your pie or your life, then!

LITTLE WOLF: No. Teaching first, pies after.

UNCLE BIGBAD: (*Pounding the table.*) Pie.

LITTLE WOLF: No –

UNCLE BIGBAD: PIE.

LITTLE WOLF: But Uncle –

UNCLE BIGBAD: (*Huffing and puffing.*) Pies you vile fluffy –

LITTLE WOLF: No!

UNCLE BIGBAD: **Sniff snuff sny**
> **Give me that mouse pie,**
> **I've got a gnawing hunger here**
> **Mice pie would satisfy.**
> **I am owed some pain relief**
> **So spike one on my sharpest teeth,**
> **I'll drop my drooling drawbridge jaw**
> **I promise I won't snap your paw**

So give me pie and see I'm fed
Or I'll bite off your head.

LITTLE WOLF: No.

UNCLE BIGBAD: Argggg! All right, all right I'll teach you bags of badness, you little sissy. (*Opening his mouth.*)

LITTLE WOLF: One rule, one pie. That's fair.

UNCLE BIGBAD: (*Drooling.*) Fair? We don't use that word in here.

LITTLE WOLF: You owe me two rules of badness.

UNCLE BIGBAD: You owe me all your pies.

LITTLE WOLF: Why? Two rules, two pies! And you've already had two.

UNCLE BIGBAD: All right, all right just give me that pie and I'll teach you.

LITTLE WOLF: Three rules of badness.

UNCLE BIGBAD: Three?

LITTLE WOLF: Yes. Three.

UNCLE BIGBAD: Very well my splendid brainy boy. Where do we start?

LITTLE WOLF gives him the pie.

Yum, yum, yigh
I love you wild mice pie,
I'm a big bad greedy wolf
And I'll be satisfied.

LITTLE WOLF: **Oh Uncle I am not a fool**
It's time you taught me those three rules,
You then can have another one
When all our lessons have begun,
I'm ready steady I could start
To learn those rules by heart

LITTLE WOLF / UNCLE BIGBAD: **Yum-my yum,**
Yum yum yum-my yum.
Yum yum yum-my yum.
No rule, no pie,

No rule, no pie.

Yum yum yum-my yum.

Arooooo!

UNCLE BIGBAD stands up and polishes his gold badge. LITTLE WOLF sits at another desk with his exercise book at the ready.

UNCLE BIGBAD: (*Finishing his pie.*) You don't look crafty enough to learn the rules of badness.

LITTLE WOLF: I am. I'm going to try my hardest.

UNCLE BIGBAD: Very well my clueless cub, let's start with a story. Two rules of badness are hidden in it. Listen: Once upon a time I lived near Three Little Piggies and they got on my nerves singing that they were not afraid of a big bad wolf. And they kept going ha-ha-ha-ha-ha all the time. So I huffed and I huffed and I puffed their houses down and ate them.

LITTLE WOLF: Were the bricks tasty?

UNCLE BIGBAD: Silence, speck, that is not funny! I once had a blasted dreadful accident with a brick house. I nearly blew my head off trying to huff it down. So blinking blunking keep quiet about brick houses!

LITTLE WOLF: Is that the story?

UNCLE BIGBAD: Yes. It's going to take you years and years to guess –

LITTLE WOLF: I think Rule One is: Huff and puff a lot; and Rule Two is: Say loads of rude words.

UNCLE BIGBAD: Cheat!

LITTLE WOLF: I didn't cheat.

UNCLE BIGBAD: Somebody must have told you those.

LITTLE WOLF: Nobody told me! I guessed. Let's do Rule Three?

UNCLE BIGBAD: You practise your huffing and puffing, you fluffball, and don't come whining for more rules until you can blow a house down!

Music

UNCLE BIGBAD flies into a rage, tips over LITTLE WOLF's desk, steals his bag of pies and leaves.

SCENE TWO

GRIZZLE in the lair. LITTLE WOLF in the classroom.

GRIZZLE: (*Reading.*) 'Uncle went mad at me for guessing Rules One and Two.'

LITTLE WOLF: Uncle, when is lunch?

GRIZZLE: Oh Little!

UNCLE BIGBAD: Lunch! Lunch! There is no food in this house. Where's my lunch, you blinking blunker? Flee and fly into Frettnin Forest and make me a squirrel burger, swiftly swiftly or you leave this school, forthwith.

GRIZZLE: (*Reading.*) 'I spent ages trying to catch squirrels but I'm hopeless at climbing trees. All I got was just some peabugs and earwigs for crunchy snacks. He ate the lot without sharing, and then went growlier and he bit a lump out of the sink.'

UNCLE BIGBAD bites a chunk out of the sink.

LITTLE WOLF cowers in a corner or leaves the room.

'That was the last lesson I got that day or the day after. I did huffing and puffing dandelions for the practice but it made me dizzy.'

LITTLE WOLF is discovered blowing dandelions. He makes himself dizzy and falls over.

'At night I must sleep in a dorm. It is a big long room with twenty beds where all the other brute beasts used to sleep before they disappeared. Sleeping in a dorm is not cosy like home. At night and when I'm writing to you, I am thinking, how come Uncle always stays so fat when there is no food here? He never does any hunting, just lies on the roof all night howling at the moon. My tummy does rumbles all night because of the hunger and it makes music with his howling –'

Music – <u>The Song of Cheesy Moon and Empty Tummy</u>

UNCLE BIGBAD on the roof. LITTLE WOLF in a dorm.

Chorus:

UNCLE BIGBAD: Aroooo!

LITTLE WOLF: Grrrow!

UNCLE BIGBAD: Arooo!

LITTLE WOLF: Grrrow!

UNCLE BIGBAD: Arooo!

LITTLE WOLF: Arooo! Howl growl!

End of chorus.

LITTLE WOLF: It's gone midnight hours ago
   And I can't get to sleep,
   Shh! hungry tum stop rumbling
   I've got no food to eat.
   If only I could fall asleep
   And dream the pain away,
   I'd eat more than three times as much
   Three times every day.

Chorus.

MOON: (*Over the chorus.*) You'll never reach me.
   You can't eat me.

UNCLE BIGBAD: Delicious moon don't be afraid for
   Surely you can see
   There's just the two of us out here
   And I'm your devotee.
   I long to kiss the smile off you
   To taste your cheesy grin,
   You're not to shy away, dear moon,
   Embrace the state I'm in.

Chorus.

LITTLE WOLF: Uncle stop that horrid din,
   You'd better give up soon,
   There's nothing out there scared of you
   Stop howling at the moon.
   I've tried hard to ignore your din
   I've tried to count black sheep
   But every ugly sound you make
   Prevents me going to sleep.

Chorus.

> *The moon teases UNCLE BIGBAD by coming closer and then retreating.*

UNCLE BIGBAD: **Cresent cheese drop down a bit**
   Relieve my agony,
   Your smile and cheesy fragrance
   Drives a he-wolf moon-crazy.
   Come close, don't tease, you naughty cheese,
   No need to be afraid.
   Come let me smooch a slice of you
   Before I go to bed!

Come on, moony, give Uncle a big cheesy mouthful.

Chorus.

> *The moon is within reach and then suddenly withdraws. UNCLE BIGBAD swipes at it and misses, howls, comes down off the roof and settles in an armchair. LITTLE WOLF goes to sleep.*

GRIZZLE: Bigbad sleeps in the morning and never gets up when you call him.

Music

SCENE THREE

UNCLE BIGBAD is discovered under a blanket on the armchair, tail on the floor, snoring. Cupboards. LITTLE WOLF standing nearby with a mallet.

LITTLE WOLF: Uncle why won't you get up and teach me?

> *He brings the mallet down on the tail.*

> *He misses – twice!*

> *On his third attempt the doorbell clangs. LITTLE WOLF answers the door. The SCOUTMASTER appears.*

SCOUTMASTER: So sorry to bother you, sonny Jim, but we are camping nearby. Could you possibly do something to mend that burglar alarm on your roof. It didn't stop all night. My poor cubs never slept a wink.

LITTLE WOLF: Flee and fly immediately! Grrr!

SCOUTMASTER: (*Without registering LITTLE WOLF's attempts to scare him.*) Thank you very much, sonny Jim, have a nice day.

SCOUTMASTER leaves.

LITTLE WOLF: Uncle, Uncle it's time to get up!

UNCLE BIGBAD: (*Groans.*)

LITTLE WOLF: A man came by with a whistle complaining about you howling and I scared him away with –

UNCLE BIGBAD: (*Groaning.*) Breakfast!

LITTLE WOLF: Teach me the next rule –

UNCLE BIGBAD: Breakfast!

Pause. UNCLE BIGBAD turns over and starts to snore again.

LITTLE WOLF tries UNCLE BIGBAD's cupboards but finds them locked. Daringly, he takes a key off UNCLE BIGBAD's belt and opens the cupboards. Finds food.

GRIZZLE: (*Reads.*) 'I found loads of food all hidden away. There was ratflakes, some dried vole, organic mouseli! Mister Twister was right, he is a miser, and given what may be, perhaps he does have some hidden treasure somewhere after all.'

UNCLE BIGBAD suddenly wakes. LITTLE WOLF hurries to tidy away the food.

UNCLE BIGBAD: What are you doing?! You blinking blunking crafty nephew! Keep out of there, you sneaker! Give me my key! That's my business. You want to learn to keep out of my business! / Those are my emergency snacks.

LITTLE WOLF: But Uncle I'm so hungry!

UNCLE BIGBAD: You're worse than the moon, and the moon's a terrible cheat.

LITTLE WOLF: How can the moon be a cheat, Uncle?

UNCLE BIGBAD: Big round cheat! I'm up there on the roof howling my head off and it's coming nearer and nearer, and getting bigger and bigger, but just when I think it's close enough to take a nice big cheesy bite out of, it backs away!

LITTLE WOLF: But you said you were up there practising your terror howls, not trying to catch a free cheesy snack. You're such a liar, Uncle. Like you said there was no food in this house and there is loads hidden away!

UNCLE BIGBAD: Clever boy!

LITTLE WOLF: What?

UNCLE BIGBAD: That's Rule Number Three.

LITTLE WOLF: What? Tell lies.

UNCLE BIGBAD: Exactly. Fib your head off to be precise.

LITTLE WOLF: Fib your head off?

UNCLE BIGBAD: Fib.

LITTLE WOLF writes it in his book.

LITTLE WOLF: Fib your head off.

UNCLE BIGBAD: Now go out and get me some breakfast or else –

LITTLE WOLF: Are you proud of me?

UNCLE BIGBAD: Go!

LITTLE WOLF: I'm going.

GRIZZLE: (*Reading.*) 'I am trying so hard to be like uncle, so you too can be proud of me. Yours craftily, L Wolf, son of Gripper the Fierce.'

Music – <u>Red Riding Hood</u>

SCENE FOUR

Frettnin Forest. Enter LITTLE RED GOODIE-HOODIE, walking purposefully. LITTLE WOLF ducks out of sight.

WOODCUTTER enters, whistles loudly. LITTLE RED GOODIE-HOODIE stops.

WOODCUTTER: You forgot your basket.

GOODIE-HOODIE: Thank you, Dad.

WOODCUTTER: You left it by the door. Tell your Nan, I'll be round to chop her firewood tomorrow. You take care now.

GOODIE-HOODIE: I will.

WOODCUTTER: Good girl.

WOODCUTTER leaves.

GOODIE-HOODIE: I am. I'm a good girl I am. Good.

Music – The Song of Little Red Goodie-Hoodie

Chorus:

GOODIE-HOODIE: **I'm Little Red Goodie-Hoodie,**
> **Ready to do good,**
> **All the goodie type of things**
> **That a goodie girl should.**

End of chorus.

> **I'm Little Red Goodie Hood.**

> **I'm well turned out, I'm clean and pressed,**
> **And smell of jasmine flower.**
> **When by bad luck I dirty up**
> **I'm first to take a shower.**

Chorus.

> **I say my please and thank you**
> **And I'm quite prepared to queue,**
> **And never stop to disagree**
> **But do what I'm told to do.**

Chorus.

> **I'm on my way to see my Nan,**
> **So old she's nearly dead,**
> **But she likes to eat a picnic**
> **While she's propped up in her bed.**

> **I'll listen to her stories**
> **And I'll smile obligingly**
> **And then I'll wash her teeth and hands,**
> **And make her a cup of tea.**

Chorus.

> **I never talk to strangers**
> **And I never take their sweets,**

For I know that if I'm really good,
My Dad will give me treats.

Chorus.

LITTLE WOLF follows LITTLE RED GOODIE-HOODIE and then pops out in front of her.

LITTLE WOLF: Do you want to play?

GOODIE-HOODIE: (*No answer.*)

LITTLE WOLF: Grrr.

GOODIE-HOODIE: I'm not scared of you.

LITTLE RED GOODIE-HOODIE turns and runs away, dropping two chicken legs from her basket.

LITTLE WOLF: Only tricking.

LITTLE WOLF picks up the chicken legs.

Yum, yum!

SCOUTMASTER appears. LITTLE WOLF hides his chicken.

SCOUTMASTER: Hello, sonny Jim, fancy meeting you again.

LITTLE WOLF: Grrr!

SCOUTMASTER: I am the leader of a pack of cub scouts. We are camping down by Lake Lemming. Tomorrow we plan to have a barbecue. We hope that you can join us. Here is an invitation.

LITTLE WOLF: Grr!

SCOUTMASTER: Oh dear, have you got a sore throat, sonny Jim? Have a cough sweet, must dash now.

Music

SCENE FIVE

Back in Cunning College. UNCLE BIGBAD's dressing room. Words written in dust on a large mirror.

UNCLE BIGBAD: **Yum, yum, yummy yum**
Yum, yum, yum,
Yum, yum yummy
Fill my tum.

> Tum tum, tummy tum
> Full of yum
> Chicken legs are
> Srumptious.

LITTLE WOLF: Yum, yum, yummy yum
> Yum, yum, yum,
> Yum, yum yummy
> Fill your tum.
> Tum tum, tummy tum
> Full of yum
> There's plenty more
> Where they come from.

TOGETHER: Chicken legs are
> Srumptious.

LITTLE WOLF: Uncle, I have written down three rules in my Book of Badness. Can you teach me Number Four?

UNCLE BIGBAD: How many more of these delicious chicken legs can I have?

LITTLE WOLF: One now, and lots more later.

UNCLE BIGBAD: Are you fibbing?

LITTLE WOLF: (*No answer.*) Um?

UNCLE BIGBAD: I adore chicken legs so I will tell you two more rules. If it squeaks, eat it.

LITTLE WOLF: Rule Number Four.

UNCLE BIGBAD: Rule Number Four. Rule Number Five: Blow everybody else.

LITTLE WOLF: Blow everybody else?

LITTLE WOLF blows.

UNCLE BIGBAD: I'm not talking about huffing and puffing, I'm talking about looking after number one, me, you, yourself. If you want to be a bad wolf, put yourself first at all times, forget everybody else.

LITTLE WOLF: Like you don't bother about me. I've been invited to a barbecue.

UNCLE BIGBAD: I'm coming.

LITTLE WOLF: But you haven't been invited.

UNCLE BIGBAD: I'm coming.

LITTLE WOLF: Only if you teach me Rule Number Six.

UNCLE BIGBAD: I'll get ready.

UNCLE BIGBAD looks at himself in mirror, thick with dust.

LITTLE WOLF: You haven't been invited.

UNCLE BIGBAD: Clean my mirror you nettle –

LITTLE WOLF: Uncle why have you written 'Do Your Dirtiest' in the mirror?

UNCLE BIGBAD: To remind me, that of all the Rules of Badness the one that matters most to a good bad wolf is Rule Number…

LITTLE WOLF: Six?

UNCLE BIGBAD: Do your dirtiest. I'm coming to that barbecue or you can leave this school…now! And your mother and father will have to deal with the shame of having their eldest cub expelled from the finest school in Beastshire –

LITTLE WOLF: It starts at five forty-eight. It's a cub scout barbecue at their camp by Lake Lemming.

UNCLE BIGBAD: Where we will do our dirtiest, my co-operative little creeper. Cub scouts… Delicious.

LITTLE WOLF: The pack leader wants us to eat his sausages not his cubs.

UNCLE BIGBAD: I know their motto is 'be prepared'. Thus and therefore I shall prepare some for the oven and the rest for the pot.

LITTLE WOLF: I'm looking forward to my sausages especially since you never let me eat any of your food.

UNCLE BIGBAD: What food?

LITTLE WOLF: The food in your cupboards.

UNCLE BIGBAD: (*Opening the cupboards.*) What food? I haven't got any food.

LITTLE WOLF: I don't believe you. You've hidden it somewhere else. Just thinking about yourself the whole time and blow everybody else, I suppose. What about my tum?

UNCLE BIGBAD: Shut up you sissy silent speck! Observe the beastliest brute beast of Beastshire and learn from the master. You wait till tomorrow, five forty-eight. Tomorrow I'll teach you Rule Seven. I'll show you how to do charming. Charming will always get you a good feed.

LITTLE WOLF: But I'm hungry, now.

UNCLE BIGBAD: (*Turning angry.*) That's enough! Go and practise your howl and growl and your huff and puff, or go to bed! Unless of course you've got any more of those chicken legs, you're hiding from me…

LITTLE WOLF hangs his head.

BED!

LITTLE WOLF leaves.

Music

GRIZZLE: (*Reading.*) 'Boo shame. Uncle is too good at doing dirty. Yours upsetly, Little.'

SCENE SIX

CUB SCOUTS establish their camp whilst singing a verse and chorus of a traditional scout song.

During the setting up of the camp, LITTLE WOLF and UNCLE BIGBAD are discovered on Windy Ridge, smiling in the face of the North Wind, teeth jittering.

LITTLE WOLF: If this is charming it's rubbish, I am frozz all over.

UNCLE BIGBAD: Stretch those lips, big smile, face the bitter north wind until it sticks…

Segue into Music – Smiles Do

UNCLE BIGBAD: When you want someone to do something
That they may not want to do,
When what you need's your enemy

To start supporting you,
Wear a smile, wear a smile,
Then like a child they'll
Do what you want
They're soon beguiled.

SCOUTS: Dyb, dyb, dob.

UNCLE BIGBAD: When you want something you cannot have
When the bargaining is through,
When you fancy someone over there,
But you're not sure they like you,
Wear a smile, wear a smile,
Then like a child they'll
Do what you want

SCOUTS: We're soon beguiled.

UNCLE BIGBAD: They're soon beguiled.

LITTLE WOLF / UNCLE BIGBAD: Wear a smile
Then like a child they'll
do what you want
They're soon beguiled

Smiles do –
Win through!

UNCLE BIGBAD: (*Between gritted teeth.*) Can you still feel the stretch?

LITTLE WOLF: I can't feel anything.

UNCLE BIGBAD: You're ready then

LITTLE WOLF nods his head.

Segue into Music

SCOUTMASTER approaches them.

SCOUTMASTER: Welcome, Sir, welcome, sonny Jim, what charming smiles. I can see we're going to be the best of friends. Would you like something to eat?

LITTLE WOLF: I would like a nice hot / sausage.

UNCLE BIGBAD: I would like your cub scouts or I'll huff and I'll puff and I'll blow their tents down.

SCOUTMASTER: (*Blowing his whistle.*)

Music

Quick! All scouts to your tents! Quick!

SCOUTMASTER, DAVE and SANJAY dive into their tents and zip them up. They are lit from within.

UNCLE BIGBAD starts to huff and puff. As he does so the tents bend away and spring back into shape, emphasizing the power of his puff.

UNCLE BIGBAD: Help me you Little –

LITTLE WOLF: (*Squeaking.*) I can't huff and puff my mouth's frozen –

UNCLE BIGBAD: (*Huffing and puffing.*) Stand by the fire you blinking – !

LITTLE WOLF: Then I'll burn myself.

UNCLE BIGBAD: **I'm a growler,**
I'm a howler,
I'm a midnight prowler,
I'm the fiercest foulest beast
You'll ever meet.

Huffs and puffs.

SCOUTS: (***From inside their tents.***) **Who's afraid of the big bad wolf,**
Big bad wolf, big bad wolf?
Who's afraid... (***Etc.***)

Spoken under chorus:

UNCLE BIGBAD: Blow, Little! Blow!

LITTLE WOLF: I may only be a learner but I can see those pegs and strings are in just right and they're not lifting –

UNCLE BIGBAD: Blow!

I'm huffer,
I'm puffer,
And you can't give me enough of
Sweating plump barbecued
Scout ribs...

Huffs and puffs.

SCOUTS: (*From inside their tents.*) **Who's afraid of the big bad wolf,
Big bad wolf, big bad wolf?
Who's afraid...** (*Etc.*)

Spoken under chorus:

LITTLE WOLF: But I only came for a sausage.

UNCLE BIGBAD: Blow!

LITTLE WOLF: Forget the cubs, Uncle, I know how you can catch a
nice tasty little girl with a red hood.

UNCLE BIGBAD: Blow!

LITTLE WOLF: Dress up as her granny! I'll lend you my bonnet.

UNCLE BIGBAD: **My hunger's rushing,
My spit is flushing,
My inner-ear can hear bones crushing
As I tear you limb by limb
For my din-dins.**

Huffs and puffs.

SCOUTS: (*From inside their tents.*) **Who's afraid of the big bad wolf,
Big bad wolf, big bad wolf?
Who's afraid...** (*Etc.*)

UNCLE BIGBAD: Help me! Come and puff, come and huff, come and
blow these tents down!

Twizzling around and around while huffing and puffing.

Blinking, (*Huff.*) blinking, (*Huff.*) blinking, (*Huff.*) blarsted!

**Without a doubt
A tasty scout
Is what this puffing's all about,
I'll huff and puff and blow
These tents away.**

Huffs and puffs.

SCOUTS: (*From inside their tents.*) **Who's afraid of the big bad wolf,
Big bad wolf, big bad wolf?
Who's afraid...** (*Etc.*)

UNCLE BIGBAD: I'm out of puff
I'm feeling rough
I think I might've had enough,
Can't seem to raise these
Peggies out the ground

Huffs and puffs.

SCOUTS: (*From inside their tents.*) Who's afraid of the big bad wolf,
Big bad wolf, big bad wolf?
Who's afraid... (*Etc.*)

UNCLE BIGBAD: (*Slowing down.*) O blinking heck
I feel a wreck
I think I'm going to hit the deck
I'll be back before –
Sweet cubs goodniiiight...

UNCLE BIGBAD collapses, banging his head.

LITTLE WOLF: Uncle I think I'm ready to puff now. Uncle?

SCOUTS: (*Emerging from their tents.*)
We're not afraid of the big sad wolf,
Big sad wolf, big sad wolf!
We're not afraid... (*Etc.*)

LITTLE WOLF pulls UNCLE BIGBAD off by the tail.

SCENE SEVEN

Music

GRIZZLE: (*Reading.*) 'I have written down Rule Seven in my Book of
Badness. This is it. Rule Seven: Do charming sneaky smiles. It is
rubbish. I had to drag Uncle all the way home by his tail. He has
a bad head and tailache. I gave him the bonnet I took from the
market. And a cunning trick jumped into my head.'

LITTLE WOLF is preparing.

LITTLE WOLF: Uncle if you pretended to be Little Red Goodie-
Hoodie's gran by wearing this bonnet I got from the market you
could eat her and forget about what happened at the barbecue.

UNCLE BIGBAD: You are the stupidest pupil I have ever had. (*A sudden idea.*) I have thought of a brilliant way to trap that little red hood girlie, wear this bonnet and pretend to be her granny.

LITTLE WOLF: That's what I said.

UNCLE BIGBAD: So what? If you were a really clever, cunning big bad wolf, you would keep your good ideas to yourself and not blab them around. Write that in your stupid book of badness. Rule Eight: Do not blab your good ideas.

As LITTLE WOLF writes Rule Eight in his book UNCLE BIGBAD dresses up.

(*Dressing up as granny.*) Yes, very nice. I think it suits me. Now take me there.

SCENE EIGHT

Segue into Music

Double location: The Lair, Murkshire, and a doorway to a small cottage in Frettnin Forest.

UNCLE BIGBAD and LITTE WOLF on their way to the cottage.

UNCLE BIGBAD: (*Practising his granny voice.*) My dear Little Red Goodie-Hoodie, come in!

YELLER and SMELLYBREFF reading letters in the lair.

YELLER: (*Reading.*) 'You should have heard Uncle's granny voice, it was rubbish! Even Smellybreff can do better voices.'

SMELLYBREFF: (*Mimicking a granny's voice.*) My dear Little Red Goodie-Hoodie, come in!

YELLER: Very good! (*Reading.*) 'At last we got going to Grandma's house about tea time.'

UNCLE BIGBAD and LITTLE WOLF arrive outside an old cottage. He knocks on the door.

'Uncle went in and had all the bad fun.'

GRANNY: (*Off.*) Come in!

UNCLE BIGBAD passes through the door. The sound of violent activity behind the door.

YELLER: (*Reading.*) 'He would not let me tie the old lady up or stick her in the wardrobe. He said my job was to stay outside and give a wolf whistle if any woodcutters came along.'

UNCLE BIGBAD: Any woodcutters, you whistle, do you hear? Like this!

UNCLE BIGBAD wolf-whistles, LITTLE WOLF copies him.

That's called a WOLF WHISTLE!

Enter LITTLE RED GOODIE-HOODIE with a basket of food. LITTLE WOLF hides. LITTLE RED GOODIE-HOODIE knocks on the door.

(*Mimicking granny, behind the door.*) It's open. Come in my dear and lock the door behind you.

LITTLE RED GOODIE-HOODIE goes in. LITTLE WOLF reappears and listens at the door.

GOODIE-HOODIE: (*From behind the door.*) Oh Granmamma what big eyes you've got!

UNCLE BIGBAD: (*From behind the door.*) All the better to see you with.

GOODIE-HOODIE: (*From behind the door.*) Oh Granmamma what big ears you've got!

UNCLE BIGBAD: (*From behind the door.*) All the better to hear you with.

GOODIE-HOODIE: (*From behind the door.*) Oh Granmamma what a big nose you've got!

UNCLE BIGBAD: (*From behind the door.*) All the better to smell you with.

GOODIE-HOODIE: (*From behind the door.*) Oh Granmamma what big teeth you've got!

UNCLE BIGBAD: (*From behind the door.*) All the better to EAT YOU WITH!

GOODIE-HOODIE: (*From behind the door, screaming.*) AHHHHH!

UNCLE BIGBAD attacks and eats LITTLE RED GOODIE-HOODIE. LITTLE WOLF hammers at the door.

YELLER / SMELLYBREFF: Hooray! Yummy yummy! (*Etc.*)

LITTLE WOLF: (*Banging at the door.*) Let me in! Uncle let me in! I'm so hungry.

UNCLE BIGBAD: (*From behind the door.*) Not by the hair of my chinny- / chin-chin!

LITTLE WOLF: Save some for me!

UNCLE BIGBAD: (*From behind the door.*) No.

LITTLE WOLF: You are so greedy!

SMELLYBREFF: What happened next?

YELLER: (*Referring back to the letter.*) Then Little Wolf went off and chased a few snacks for his tea in the forest. 'But while I was chasing snacks the woodcutter must've come along and whacked Uncle on the bonnet with the back of his axe. Also he split him in two and rescued Red Goodie-Hoodie out of his tummy and Granmamma from the cupboard. He made me sew him up.'

Music

SCENE NINE

LITTLE WOLF appears wrapping UNCLE BIGBAD's head in vinegar-soaked strips of brown paper.

UNCLE BIGBAD: You stupid, stupid Little Wolf! I told you. Didn't I tell you, stay by the door and wolf-whistle if you saw a woodcutter?

LITTLE WOLF: But I couldn't help it, I was hungry. I think you should see a doctor, Uncle.

UNCLE BIGBAD: How can I afford a doctor when I have to pay to look after you?

LITTLE WOLF: My Dad gave you a cheque.

UNCLE BIGBAD: Keep the flies off, they're driving me mad!

LITTLE WOLF swats UNCLE BIGBAD on the head and causes him more pain.

Ow! You idiot!

If you want to help me you can write me a letter to my friend Mr Twister.

LITTLE WOLF: Your friend?

Segue into Music

SMELLYBREFF: I thought Uncle Bigbad hated Mister Twister?

YELLER: Not as much as he hates Little, by the looks of things. He
needs help.

LITTLE WOLF taking dictation from UNCLE BIGBAD.

Letter to Mr Twister

UNCLE BIGBAD: **My dearest long-lost Twister are you well?**
I'm writing in the hopes time has dispelled
All the minor differences we had while you were here,
I hope you might return and claim your share.

I'll pay you handsomely, unlike before,
And promise you no routine, no boring chores,
No teaching brutes, and registers and sports on first
Wednesdays,
I promise you I'll give you a fair say.

You let my stupid nephew work your stall,
It's all his blinking fault I'm at death's door,
He let a blarsted woodcutter bonk-bash my sleek grey head,
And leave me belly-split in bed for dead.

LITTLE WOLF: Liar. I haven't eaten anything for days.

UNCLE BIGBAD: **If you could nurse me through this then I could**
Take myself away from Frettnin wood
We could buy a hilltop farm together and worry stupid sheep,
Be mutually dependent for our keep.

Your melancholy friend implores your aid,
If you had muzzled me, you might've stayed,
You'd have kept my pupil quotas up and made sure they all
paid,
I've lost a blinking fortune, I'm afraid.

LITTLE WOLF: That's not true.

UNCLE BIGBAD signs letter.

YELLER: 'B B Wolf.'

SMELLYBREFF: B? B?

YELLER: Bigbad.

UNCLE BIGBAD: (*To LITTLE WOLF.*) Now you can blinking blunkin well buzz off. I'm too poor to keep you.

LITTLE WOLF: But Uncle I've only got one more rule to learn and then I will leave you alone.

UNCLE BIGBAD: Get out, you are much too expensive for me.

LITTLE WOLF: How can you say that? You've spent nothing on me. You're a big miser.

UNCLE BIGBAD: What did you say?

LITTLE WOLF: Mister Twister told me.

UNCLE BIGBAD: That's a flippin floppin whopping lie!!! Mister Twister told you I've bags of gold stuffed up the…

LITTLE WOLF: Up the what?

UNCLE BIGBAD: Get out of here! Out, do you hear? OUT OF MY SIGHT!

He exits.

YELLER: (*Reading letter.*) 'So, now I'm all on my own in Frettnin Forest again. Yours chucked-outly, L Wolf.'

SMELLYBREFF: What about his badge?

YELLER: He can't come home without a badge. Your Dad won't let him.

Music – <u>Shadow Song</u>

LITTLE WOLF alone talking to his shadow.

LITTLE WOLF: **Forgive and forget me**
 I'm not coming home,
 I'll stay in the forest
 And live on my own,
 My sad yellow eyes
 Will make friends of the dark,
 I'm a Little Bad Wolf
 Who didn't make the mark.

I've let you all down
Especially Dad
'Cause I've messed up on all
Of the chances I had.
I worked very hard
But the going was tough
And I only learned eight rules
And eight ain't enough.

Whatever I do,
I'm in the wrong.
Wherever I roam
I'm not free,
So, I'm changing me name
To be somebody else,
I'll be the shadow
That's following me

My shadow, my shadow
That's who I'll be,
I'll be my own shadow
And stop being
ME!

UNCLE BIGBAD comes back.

UNCLE BIGBAD: Still here? I'll give you one more chance. If you can pass the big survival test, I'll give you Rule Nine and a badge.

LITTLE WOLF: I have already passed, haven't I? Living with you?

UNCLE BIGBAD: You must stay alive in Frettnin Forest with no shelter, no provisions, no nothing for a week. And at the end of that week you must bring me back something big and lipsmackerous to eat.

LITTLE WOLF: How am I supposed to do that?

UNCLE BIGBAD: Oh, and while you're about it, post this letter for me!

LITTLE WOLF: It will be too hard for me, Uncle.

UNCLE BIGBAD: Please yourself.

UNCLE BIGBAD leaves.

LITTLE WOLF: All right then. I will have a go.

SCENE TEN

YELLER: (*Reading a letter.*) 'Do not worry. I am not coming home badgeless. You will be proud of me. I shall look for a cave, without a grizzly bear in it, to live in, and I shall snack on hedgehogs if I have to.'

Music

LITTLE WOLF walking through the forest. It is windy, it is raining. LITTLE WOLF getting weaker and weaker...tries to pounce on a bird and misses, tries to eat a hedgehog but it hurts, tries to cover himself in leaves but they keep falling off him. So he covers his eyes in leaves.

Enter SANJAY and DAVE. They discover LITTLE WOLF.

SANJAY: Hello Little Wolf.

DAVE: Are you all right?

SANJAY: Can we help?

DAVE: You are as skinny as a rake.

LITTLE WOLF: (*Faintly.*) I'm all right.

SANJAY: You don't sound all right.

LITTLE WOLF: I –

DAVE: We'll soon fatten you up.

LITTLE WOLF: (*Trying to move away, but too weak.*) And make a stew of me.

LITTLE WOLF collapses.

Music – A version of 'Dyb, dyb, dob'

Enter SCOUTMASTER and CUB SCOUTS. In a series of tableaux, LITTLE WOLF is fed, groomed, rested and introduced to the life of a cub scout.

LITTLE WOLF: All this food is lipsmackerous, especially the baked beans.

SCOUTMASTER: You are not like other wolves. You are not a bad fellow. Perhaps you'd like to join our pack and work for a badge or two. You could start with your Reader's Badge, or maybe your Animal Lover's –

LITTLE WOLF: I love rabbit rolls.

SCOUTMASTER: Animal Lover's is not an eating badge.

LITTLE WOLF: Yes but first I must get my Bad Badge.

SCOUTMASTER: Bad Badge?

LITTLE WOLF: There are Nine Rules of Badness but I only know eight. Uncle Bigbad says he will tell me Number Nine if I can survive a week in the forest and bring him back something lipsmackerous to eat. If you tell me –

SCOUTMASTER: Haven't a clue.

LITTLE WOLF: (*Counting on his claws.*) Huff and puff a lot. / Say loads of rude words.

SCOUTMASTER: Wouldn't know where to begin.

LITTLE WOLF: Fib your head off. Blow everyone else. If it squeaks eat it. Do your dirtiest every day…

SCOUTMASTER: Do charming?

LITTLE WOLF: Do charming. Do not blab your good ideas.

SCOUTMASTER: You see, scout rules are the opposite.

LITTLE WOLF: That's only eight.

SANJAY: Do your best.

DAVE: Think of others.

SANJAY: Do good turns.

SCOUTMASTER: Your Uncle is a cruel savage brute.

LITTLE WOLF: Uncle would be so happy to hear you call him that.

SCOUTMASTER: You're the first real wolf cub we have met that has ever wanted to be friends.

LITTLE WOLF: Mum and Dad say I need to be bad enough to stop human people making me into slippers.

SCOUTMASTER: Sonny Jim, if I talk to the fur-hunters will you talk to your Uncle for me? There must be a way we can share this magnificent forest, and all the adventures therein, without being frightened of one another.

LITTLE WOLF: He won't listen.

SCOUTMASTER: Not even if you take him some chocolate fingers and potty noodles?

LITTLE WOLF: Maybe.

SCOUTMASTER: Go on then.

LITTLE WOLF: What about if the hunters don't listen to you?

SCOUTMASTER: Slippers don't need to be made of fur.

LITTLE WOLF: What about coats?

SCOUTMASTER: Or coats. Now before you leave, let me say: Little Wolf, you have made the last few days here very special for us at Lakeside Camp. We are proud to be part of your great adventure, and thus and therefore, we would like to make you a presentation. So here is your Special Cub Scout Adventure Award with certificate and badge.

LITTLE WOLF: Wow! And I thought my first badge would be a bad one.

SCOUTMASTER: And here are some provisions for a safe journey back to Cunning College and one or two things to remind you of our time together when you get back to Murkshire. And remember you will always be welcome at the Lakeside Camp.

Music

In turn, the SCOUTS present LITTLE WOLF with chocolate fingers, pot noodles, biscuits etc. and, finally, three whacking big tins of baked beans. LITTLE WOLF wraps them in a blanket and leaves. The camp disappears. Blackout.

Music – Twister Disguises

SCENE ELEVEN

Cunning College. Enter MR TWISTER disguised as a doctor.

UNCLE BIGBAD: Oh, doctor, doctor, have you come to make me better?

MR TWISTER: Show me where it hurts –

UNCLE BIGBAD: All over, doctor, all over!

MR TWISTER: Let's see if I can't make it hurt some more.

UNCLE BIGBAD: Arggh!

> *While winding a stretch bandage around and around UNCLE BIGBAD:*

MR TWISTER: **From everything that I can see,**
My hurt's much worse than yours.
You couch here in the lap of luxury;
I've had to live for years and years
In abject poverty
Because you were
So bad and miserly.

UNCLE BIGBAD: It hurts all over!

MR TWISTER: **When I have to save a patient**
But I know that secretly
Lycanthropy deserves my cruelty.
This is Twister's bold revenge, Bigbad,
For all the misery.
Give me all your gold,
To set you free!

UNCLE BIGBAD: You are not a doctor?

MR TWISTER: (*Revealing his true self.*) No, I'm a master of disguise!

UNCLE BIGBAD: (*Terrified.*) Arggh!

MR TWISTER: You miserable, merciless miser! Tell me where you've hidden my money.

UNCLE BIGBAD: My dear long-lost chum, didn't you get my letter?

MR TWISTER: I'd rather be followed by a pack of hounds than go into business with you again. Give me the money you owe me!

UNCLE BIGBAD: I haven't got any money! / Have pity on a poor wolf.

MR TWISTER: I don't believe you.

UNCLE BIGBAD: I don't owe you any money! / Help!

MR TWISTER: Yes you do!

UNCLE BIGBAD: (*Howling.*) Help! Untie me!

MR TWISTER: It's here somewhere. I know it is.

UNCLE BIGBAD: You blinking blunker, Twister. Don't wreck my school! You'll pay for this! HELP!

MR TWISTER leaves UNCLE BIGBAD all trussed up, whimpering. The sound of a school being turned upside down.

Music

SCENE TWELVE

The Lair, Murkshire. GRIZZLE reading LITTLE WOLF's latest letter to SMELLYBREFF.

GRIZZLE: 'I am deep in the forest where it is so dark and dismal you would not believe! Even the bats wear glasses (only kidding).'

SMELLYBREFF: Is he scared, Mum?

GRIZZLE: No he's not scared because the cub scouts have taught him how to make an excellent shelter out of sticks and leaves called a bivouac.

SMELLYBREFF: Can I be a cub scout?

GRIZZLE: (*Reading.*) 'I am just waiting till midnight so that I can creep back to Cunning College and surprise Uncle. Because I have passed my big test. I am still alive after a week, and I have got some lipsmackerous stuff for him to eat.'

SMELLYBREFF: Crafty Little!

Music

SCENE THIRTEEN

Cunning College. LITTLE WOLF discovers UNCLE BIGBAD all trussed up.

LITTLE WOLF: Hello Uncle.

UNCLE BIGBAD: Where've you been you little squirt? / Never here when you're needed –

LITTLE WOLF: I was doing what you told me to do.

UNCLE BIGBAD: Untie me swiftly, swiftly! That blinking blunker Mister Twister tried to squeeze the life out of me, he was after my money but I wouldn't tell him where it was hidden.

LITTLE WOLF: So you have hidden it.

UNCLE BIGBAD: Rule Nine.

LITTLE WOLF: Be a miser.

UNCLE BIGBAD: Wrong!

LITTLE WOLF: And I thought you were poor.

UNCLE BIGBAD: Do you want your badge, you little squirt? Do you want your parents to be proud of you?

LITTLE WOLF: Yes, Uncle… / very much, Uncle.

UNCLE BIGBAD: Then listen! Mind your own business and do as you're told, untie me. NOW!

LITTLE WOLF: (*Untying him.*) I've done everything you told me to and brought you something lipsmackerous to eat.

UNCLE BIGBAD: What a magnificent little pupil you are.

LITTLE WOLF: (*Opening his blanket full of provisions.*) But you will have to promise not to frighten the scouts again!

UNCLE BIGBAD: Of course, of course!

LITTLE WOLF: But how can I tell whether you are fibbing or not?

UNCLE BIGBAD: I promise, I promise!

LITTLE WOLF: You better.

Split location. Back in the lair:

GRIZZLE: 'First I gave him all my chocolate fingers.'

LITTLE WOLF feeds UNCLE BIGBAD his chocolate fingers.

UNCLE BIGBAD: I'm still hungry.

GRIZZLE: 'Then I gave him all my potty noodles. He was such a greedy guts he didn't bother to cook them or take them out of their plastic potties.'

UNCLE BIGBAD: (*Finishing off some pot noodles.*) I'm still hungry.

LITTLE WOLF: (*Lifting canteen-sized baked bean cans out of his rucksack.*) I was saving the biggest one of these for Mum and Dad and Smells, and the second biggest for Yeller for saving my life, and the smallest one for me, because Akela said I had acquired a taste for beans, and it was difficult to do without once one had acquired a taste for something.

UNCLE BIGBAD: Goody goody. Put them in the big pot. Fill it to the brim.

LITTLE WOLF opens and pours one can of beans into the pot.

To the brim.

LITTLE WOLF opens another can.

To the brimmy, brim, brim!

LITTLE WOLF opens a third can.

SMELLYBREFF: Greedy Uncle!

LITTLE WOLF puts the pot on the fire.

UNCLE BIGBAD: Feed me! Spoon them in!

LITTLE WOLF: But they won't even be warm yet.

UNCLE BIGBAD: Swiftly, swiftly! Spoon! Spoon!

Feeding Music

LITTLE WOLF feeds UNCLE BIGBAD some beans.

Nice. Very nice. More!

LITTLE WOLF: Uncle, the label says, 'Don't eat too fast. Beware of the jumping beanbangs!'

UNCLE BIGBAD: Who cares about blunking blarsted beanbangs! Feed me, feed me, swiftly swiftly! Ladle!

LITTLE WOLF: Uncle can I have Rule Nine can I have my badge –

UNCLE BIGBAD: Beans! Beans! Beans! Use the ladle! I've got a hunger on me like a –

LITTLE WOLF starts shovelling him full of beans.

UNCLE BIGBAD: Be a bad wolf and pour them down my throat –

LITTLE WOLF: But –

UNCLE BIGBAD: Go on or I'll eat you!

LITTLE WOLF: Number Nine?

UNCLE BIGBAD: Rule Number Nine: Never trust a big bad wolf!

LITTLE WOLF: Never trust a big bad wolf. Yippee! I've won a Bad Badge!

UNCLE BIGBAD grabs the pot himself and swallows the contents.

UNCLE BIGBAD: (*Collapsing in the armchair.*) I'm going to bed!

SMELLYBREFF: / Yippee!

GRIZZLE: Oh no!

UNCLE BIGBAD: Turn the light out.

LITTLE WOLF: Where's my badge?

UNCLE BIGBAD: You're wasting electricity.

LITTLE WOLF: But you promised, Uncle.

UNCLE BIGBAD: Bad wolves break promises. Bad night.

LITTLE WOLF: (*Turning out the light.*) And the same to you!

Darkness. LITTLE WOLF is seen writing a letter by the light of his torch.

In the darkness UNCLE BIGBAD releases a rip-roaring fart.

GRIZZLE: (*Reading from the letter.*) 'A whole night and a day has passed since I started this letter. Because of what has happened I think this will be my longest and my last letter. Last night while I was writing and feeling very sad and down and dumpy…Uncle had a slight accident.' Fetch your father for me, Smells.

SMELLYBREFF: What happened to Uncle, Mum?

GRIZZLE: Fetch your father, quick!

SMELLYBREFF: He's out hunting.

Another rip-roaring fart.

Music – <u>The Jumping Beanbangs</u>

LITTLE WOLF: Uncle, it said on the tin: 'Beware the jumping beanbangs.'

UNCLE BIGBAD: **I'm lying under my sheet,**
And the bad smells smell sweet,
When I'm blown to my feet –
Bang bang,
Do the jumping beanbang,
Bang bang.

I'm stretching out my sharp claws,
I've got the jitter jut jaw
I grab my bum with my paws –
Bang bang,
Do the jumping beanbang,
Bang bang.

Lights up.

There's a wind in my tum,
Popping out of my bum,
Like I'm firing a gun –
Bang bang,
Do the jumping beanbang,
Bang bang.

UNCLE BIGBAD is propelled around the round in the most elaborate,
ungainly dance. LITTLE WOLF has to avoid being downwind of UNCLE
BIGBAD, and avoid getting in his way – this gives the appearance that
he too is dancing.

TOGETHER: **Bang-a-dee bang,**
Bang bang,
A bang-a-dee bang,
Bang, bang, bang, bang,
A bang-a-dee bang,
Bang, bang!
Bang-a-dee bang,
BANG! BANG!

UNCLE BIGBAD: **I could blow down the door,**
I could strip the décor

I could float off the floor –
Bang bang,
Do the jumping beanbang,
Bang bang.

I could have me a laugh,
Squeezin' out the bad draft,
Blowin' bubbles in the bath –
Bang bang,
Do the jumping beanbang,
Bang bang.

I'm feeling precocious
With my bum halitosis,
Don't the kid-wolf dare notice –
Bang bang,
Do the jumping beanbang,
Bang bang.

TOGETHER: Bang-a-dee bang,
Bang bang,
A bang-a-dee bang,
Bang, bang, bang, bang,
A bang-a-dee bang,
Bang, bang!
Bang-a-dee bang,
BANG! BANG!

UNCLE BIGBAD: My relief turns to pain,
And I can't take the strain,
As the wind rounds again –
Bang, bang
Do the jumping beanbang,
Bang bang.

Give me something to stop
The kerbing ker-kerpop
Or I'll dance till I drop –
Bang bang,
Do the jumping beanbang,
Bang bang.

LITTLE WOLF: If you ate more than your share
   I said Uncle beware,
   You said you didn't care –
   Bang bang,
   Do the jumping beanbang,
   Bang bang.

UNCLE BIGBAD: If I can see through this smog,
   I'm going to fetch me a log
   To plug my bum with, you dog –
   Bang, bang
   Do the jumping beanbang,
   Bang bang.

LITTLE WOLF: Uncle don't be insane
   Don't go near naked flame,
   It's the beans you should blame –
   Bang, bang
   Do the jumping beanbang,
   Bang bang.

TOGETHER: Bang-a-dee bang,
   Bang bang,
   A bang-a-dee bang,
   Bang, bang, bang, bang,
   A bang-a-dee bang,
   Bang, bang!
   Bang-a-dee bang,
   BANG! BANG!

   UNCLE BIGBAD explodes into many pieces.

LITTLE WOLF: Now, I'm feeling glad,
   No, I'm not feeling sad,
   Because you were so bad.
   Uncle Bigbad
   Greedy Uncle Bigbad
   Bang bang
   Bang-a-dee bang,
   BANG BAD!

GRIPPER: He exploded.

SMELLYBREFF exits.

GRIZZLE: That's what it says here, 'Kerblaaaam'. Pieces of Uncle Bigbad scattered far and wide like the skin of a balloon.

LITTLE WOLF finds a bag of gold in the fireplace.

'And the chimney cracked and bags and bags of gold coins fell out. Now we are going to be rich and Dad can stop moaning. I have found Uncle's gold badge and awarded it to myself.'

LITTLE WOLF finds the Bad Badge and pins it on his chest.

LITTLE WOLF: Little Bad Wolf!

It starts to snow.

GRIZZLE: 'Do not worry, I shall be home soon. I am nearly ready but not quite. Yours deservingly, L B Wolf.' 'B' for 'Bad', get it?

SCOUTMASTER: Hello sonny Jim, are you all right? We heard a loud explosion and wondered what had happened?

LITTLE WOLF: Uncle was doing the jumpin beanbangs too close to the fire and blew himself to pieces.

SCOUTMASTER: Is that your badge?

LITTLE WOLF: It's a gold one.

SCOUTMASTER: Little?

LITTLE WOLF: Yes, Scoutmaster.

SCOUTMASTER: Is that your Uncle's badge?

LITTLE WOLF: Yes. Now I'm as bad as he was.

SCOUTMASTER: Are you? Are you really as bad as that?

LITTLE WOLF: Yes.

SCOUTMASTER: So you want to grow up a horrible old wolf, that nobody trusts, without any friends…living all alone?

LITTLE WOLF: No.

SCOUTMASTER: Well then, sonny Jim, don't pretend to be, or one day you'll wake up and find out that's who you are.

LITTLE WOLF: I'm not a big bad wolf, but a Little Bad Wolf.

SCOUTMASTER: And just a little bit bad.

LITTLE WOLF: Yes, but will Mum and Dad still be proud of me if I'm a little bit bad?

SCOUTMASTER: What would make them especially proud would be to see you forge your own way in the world. What say you to this: now that Cunning College is no more, you could be using some of your Uncle's money to start your own academy.

LITTLE WOLF: What's an academy?

SCOUTMASTER: It's another word for college, or school.

LITTLE WOLF: What for?

SCOUTMASTER: Not for being bad or good, but for what you like doing best.

LITTLE WOLF: For having adventures and writing about them.

SCOUTMASTER: It could be called Little Wolf's Adventure Academy.

LITTLE WOLF: Little Bad Wolf's Adventure Academy.

SCOUTMASTER: And the Lakeside Camp would come and camp on the lawn –

LITTLE WOLF: And Smellybreff and Yeller could be teachers, teaching tricks and planning adventures, and Mum and Dad could come and happy hibernate in the warm stinky cellars –

SCOUTMASTER: Well done.

Music

> **Well done!**
> **Well done, sonny Jim, well done!**
> **There's good and bad in everyone,**
> **The choice is yours, my son,**
> **Well done!**
> **Well done, sonny Jim, well done!**
> **As you reach the end of one adventure**
> **A new one's just begun,**
> **Well done!**

LITTLEWOLF: (*Writing a letter.*)
> **Dear Mum,**
> **Dear Mum, Smellybreff, dear Dad,**
> **I've learned to be the wolf I am,**